D1479117

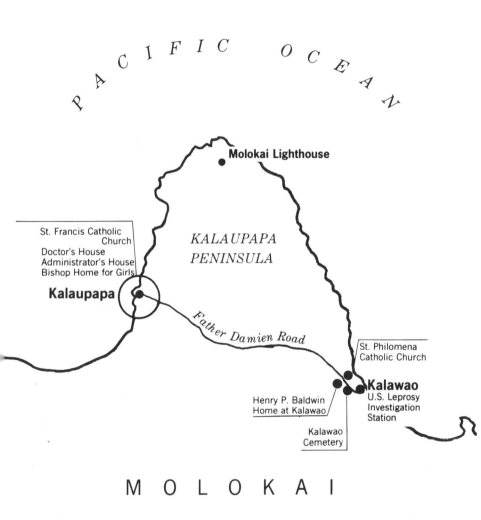

PACIFIC OCEAN

● Molokai Lighthouse

KALAUPAPA PENINSULA

St. Francis Catholic Church
Doctor's House
Administrator's House
Bishop Home for Girls

Kalaupapa

Father Damien Road

St. Philomena Catholic Church

Kalawao
U.S. Leprosy Investigation Station

Henry P. Baldwin Home at Kalawao

Kalawao Cemetery

M O L O K A I

0   ½   1   1½   2

Scale in Miles

AFTER DAMIEN:
DUTTON

Yankee Soldier at Molokai

For those who would dismiss the plight of countless
thousands upon thousands of innocent victims
of a cruel stigmatizing disease as belonging
to the pages of antiquity.

AFTER DAMIEN:
DUTTON

Yankee Soldier at Molokai

A Biographical Novel

ß
Dut

HOWARD E. CROUCH
(The Sergeant)

and

SISTER MARY AUGUSTINE, S.M.S.M.
(The Nun)

Published by the
Damien-Dutton Society for Leprosy Aid, Inc.
616 Bedford Avenue
Bellmore, New York 11710

International Standard Book Number: 0-9606330-0-6
Library of Congress Catalog Card Number: 81-67534
Published by Damien-Dutton Society for Leprosy Aid, Inc.
616 Bedford Avenue, Bellmore, N.Y. 11710
Printed in the United States of America

RL-1832

Dedication

THERE HAVE BEEN MANY OVER THE YEARS

IN RESEARCH LABS AND IN FAR-OFF MISSION WARDS

GENEROUSLY GIVING OF THEIR TIME AND TALENT TO THE ALLEVIATION

OF THE SUFFERINGS OF TODAY'S COUNTLESS VICTIMS OF LEPROSY.

ONE WHO HAS CAUGHT THE SPIRIT OF BOTH DAMIEN AND DUTTON,

REVEREND MONSIGNOR LOUIS J. MENDELIS, S.T.D., LL.D.

PASTOR EMERITUS

ST. ALPHONSUS CHURCH, BALTIMORE, MARYLAND,

IN AN APOSTOLATE UNIQUE TO HIM, ALONE AND UNAIDED,

AND IN ADDITION TO THE DEMANDS OF HIS PRIESTLY DUTIES,

HAS, DURING A LIFETIME OF SERVICE,

COLLECTED WELL OVER A MILLION DOLLARS

THAT THIS GREAT WORK MAY CONTINUE.

TO HIM, AND WITH GREAT AFFECTION,

THIS BOOK IS RESPECTFULLY DEDICATED.

Contents

Picture Credits

Acknowledgments

We have so many to thank for their help and cooperation in the writing of this book . . . many who have gone before us but have left their material on Brother Dutton either in letters or books.

For the living we are most grateful to Mrs. Betty Campbell, Mrs. Ellen Russo, Mrs. Betty Lanigan and Mr. Thomas Bluni of the Damien-Dutton Society staff for their efforts in the preparation of the manuscript. But most of all we are thankful to Rhoda Van der Clute for her comments and expertise in the technical preparation of the book itself. She is a treasured friend.

Prologue

He awoke with a start. What was it? A vague sense of something pending. What did he have to do? Fumbling for his shoes in the half-light of early morning, he suddenly remembered. O Lord in Heaven, he sighed, shaking out his shoes for any possible insects, a habit second nature to him after twenty years in the tropics. Slipping on the right shoe, he noted dully that it seemed tighter than yesterday. My poor people, he worried, passing his hands through his hair. How can I tell them! He flexed his knuckles, feeling the stiff, swollen fingers. He couldn't put it off any longer.

His clothes were damp and musty. It was going to be a steaming day, but he paid scant heed to it, his mind still taken up with what he had to put into words, for himself as well as for his congregation. Would they be surprised? Why should they, he thought. Why should anyone be surprised! Had he not been living with them for ten years now, sharing their deprivations, comforting the sick, burying the dead? Maybe if I could have had someone to help me, it would have been different! Ever honest with himself, he discounted the idea immediately. Don't fool yourself, Damien, my man, he chided himself. The ones that came were impossible, yes, wanting to do things their way, watching every little thing, eternally criticizing. But face it, who could stand a bear like me! Well, soon they will have to send someone. But where will they find a man willing to take up and stay to finish what I have started!

Shaking his head despairingly, he groped for his Breviary, opened it and strained to find his place. Yes, it was the first Sunday in June, 1885! Where had the years gone! It was a full ten years since he, as a young man of 33, had first stepped ashore at Molokai. What tragedy and heartbreak, what filth and abomination it had been at first. But all the years of hard work, all the loneliness and misunderstandings, all the constant bullying of authorities for what was needed had not been in vain. He smiled in grim satisfaction, jammed his battered hat on his head and stepped out onto the porch.

"Ready, Father?" Himano, bless his soul, was waiting. He was a quiet, diffident lad who seemed ever at hand, like a shadow, serving his Mass, running his errands, saying little, his eyes speaking volumes. Today those eyes were full of concern. Am I failing so fast, the priest wondered grumpily. A sudden thought: perhaps they have already guessed?

He leaned heavily on the willing shoulder of the boy. Where was that confounded stave he had fashioned for those long treks over the mountain path before he had cajoled the men into building the road? He was going to have to use it now, instead of burdening this frail lad.

They passed the flourishing garden, then the small cemetery. It was but a few steps more to the sacristy. He washed his hands and vested slowly, his fingers awkwardly twisting the cincture which of late was becoming increasingly difficult to manage. He prayed silently.

"Gird my loins, O Lord," and thought wryly of the biblical admonition that "the day will come when another will gird thee and lead thee where thou wouldst not." This is not of my choosing, he thought, still wrestling with the finality of his situation. Yet I have been ready for it all these years. Himano, noticing his abstraction, helped silently as the priest struggled with the chasuble.

Outside, in the eaves overhead, the soft coos of the mourning doves began their matins. A vagrant breeze wafted in the fragrant smell of honeysuckle and jasmine. Imperceptibly and then as irresistibly as the first light of the rising sun on the horizon, a ray of peace flooded his soul. He turned to the waiting Himano. "Come, my friend," he said, "This is the day the Lord hath made. Let us rejoice and be glad therein." Pulling the cord which set the bell tinkling to announce that Mass would begin, they walked slowly to the foot of the altar. "I will go unto the Altar of my God," the priest intoned, "To God Who giveth joy to my youth!"

There was a brief pause as he turned to face the congregation, each member so much a part of him. The church was filled almost to overflowing. All were neat and clean. A few had light scarves partially hiding some of their disfigurements. The eyes of all, even the blind, were fixed on the face of their priest, their friend, their father. They sensed the subtle change in him. His gaze passed slowly over each, lingering on some. The moment seemed suspended in time. They looked questioningly at each other, and back to him, reassured somewhat by the semblance of a smile on his face.

Then, with deliberateness and with great love, he opened wide his arms and began, not with his usual "My brethren," but words which would echo in their hearts and throughout the island, to ring resoundingly and reach around the world: "WE lepers . . . "

Book One

———•———

Before Damien:
War to Peace

I

Standing motionless at the rail of the small steamer approaching the bleak shores of Molokai, Joseph Dutton quietly and soberly scanned the terrain of what was to be his home, his chosen Gethsemani. The pale disc of the waning moon lingered in the silvery sky, barely distinguishable from the molten gray moving swells of the early morning sea. The steep black cliffs towered menacingly, the raucous gulls shrieking as they circled and dipped. This was the end of his long journey, and the end, too, of all that went before. This was his day of destiny.

The night had been one of pandemonium and unrelieved horror. He had hoped to forget the old tragedies of the battlefield, the cries of bereaved mothers and wives. Searching the smouldering rubble of war for the bodies of the dead abandoned in the last frantic days of the war between the States was nothing compared to accompanying these "living dead" on this voyage from which there could be no return. Fifty protesting, despairing victims had been prodded aboard, some hobbling up the gangplank unaided, others borne on canvas stretchers; all herded ruthlessly into crowded, dirty quarters, "good enough" for those considered by the world to be unclean.

For the moment there was a blessed quiet, broken only by the sloshing slap of the swells cresting at the side of the bobbing steamer. The beads of his rosary slipped through his fingers, one by one, the Sorrowful Mysteries taking on a deeper meaning as a kaleidoscope of unforgettable scenes of this voyage flashed before his mind's eye, fading, regrouping, but always in a pattern of despair. One scene kept reappearing. At the wharf, a poignantly beautiful mother, her flower-like face tight with rebellion and grief, struggled to keep her five-year-old son, who was pulled from her arms and handed over to a withered old woman with disfigured features, leaving no doubt as to the ultimate fate of the child. He thought of his own mother, long years before, who had tried so determinedly to keep him at her side, and realized anew what it must have cost her to let others guide his growing years. Mother of God, he mused, all mothers share in your loss of the Child in the Temple! As with Mary, he locked this scene in his heart.

"You can come back with me, sir! It's not too late to change your mind!"

Dutton, startled, turned to face the gruff, weather-beaten captain. He had thought the man to be without feeling, hardened against the sufferings of so many.

"No," he replied, giving the man a small nod of appreciation. "I have come too far to go back now."

The captain was not convinced.

"I wouldn't blame you, you know. No one would blame you. There's no end to all of this." And he spread his hands in disgust.

"How long before we put ashore?" Dutton queried, glancing at his unfinished rosary.

In answer the man pointed to the inhospitable shore, the frothing spume breaking relentlessly against the low-lying craggy rocks.

"It'll be another hour or so, come sunrise and getting these people together."

Arms akimbo, the man surveyed with distaste the little groups of tattered, exhausted passengers, the children still blessedly asleep.

"We can't really put ashore, y'know."

He grinned at Dutton's inquiring look, seemingly enjoying the situation.

"No ship can put ashore here, though there's a wharf of sorts. But at Kalawao where this scum is going, you couldn't even get a dinghy in. So we'll put you off here at Kalaupapa, the clean side. Then you'll have another two miles around the mountain to where you'll be living, if you stay that long."

"No," he continued, "we'll get as close as it is safe, and after that it is up to you and the dinghy. But it's not too hard. You count the waves and on the third one, you jump for it! Most of 'em make it," he added laconically.

He looked sharply at Dutton. "Once you're over at Kalawao, you won't be welcome on this side, you know." He started below, calling back over his shoulder. "Remember," he warned, "it's a sight easier to get in than to get back out!"

Dutton shuddered. Was there no end to man's inhumanity to man. He turned back to the sullen waters, opalescent now in the roseate glow on the horizon. The sound of a bell drifted across the misty waters, a mournful sort of welcome. Was that Damien's church? But no, the captain had said that Damien's settlement was on the other side of the mountain.

It was July 29, 1886. He reflected that it was more than a year since the news that the self-exiled priest at Molokai had contracted leprosy. He had read about it with growing excitement while in New Orleans. He could still feel the sense of certainty that had gripped him at the time. This was his answer, he knew without a doubt. He had won his battle against his weakness, thanks be to God, but the answer to what next had eluded him. It was one thing to "get religion," but quite another thing to grow in one's love of God.

He was on his last decade of his rosary now—the Fifth Sorrowful Mystery. He recited by rote—the fruit of the mystery: love of God's service. That's what it is all about, he decided. One can't just love God in the abstract. To love God was to love His creation, all of it, serving the neediest, the least lovable. The odyssey which had led him from the drinking halls of Nashville to the waters of Baptism had led him on to the silent corridors of a Trappist cloister, but always, peace had eluded him. Now he was at the end of the road. But not the end, he assured himself, slipping his rosary into his pocket. This was not really the end, but the beginning. And as he made the sign of the cross ending his prayers, far away, around the mountain in the little church in Kalawao, another man had finished his Mass, genuflecting painfully, to kiss the crucifix, not knowing that aboard the steamer due at Kalaupapa that morning, there was the answer to his prayer. For him, too, this was a day of destiny where the end was a new beginning.

II

It was fully daylight now. Aboard the steamer rocking slowly at anchor, all was feverish activity. Dutton, canvas knapsack in hand, waited by the rail. In the strong sunlight, the black cliffs had changed to copper, purple, mauve and blue. His trained quartermaster's eye gauged them speculatively—a good 3,000 feet high, if they are a foot, he decided. The mist had dispersed. The sky was now a wedgwood blue, the ocean shimmering and diamond-flecked. It was hard to reconcile such lush beauty with the stench and misery aboard. The children, awake and wailing, heightened the apprehension on every face. In two's and three's they were herded to the rails.

Dutton strained for some sign of what might be Damien on the distant shore. Maybe it was the figure getting down from the horse-drawn rig. Supported by a staff, the man seemed quite feeble.

"Perhaps you'd like to go first?"

The captain was brusque. Obviously this man in faded blue denims was either a dreamer or a fool. From the size and apparent lightness of his bag, he hardly had a change of clothes. He'd get tired of it soon enough, he'd wager. It's one thing for priests to get messed up in all this—but a layman! You'd have to pay plenty to get this ol' captain on that island, he thought. Well, let the man find out for himself. There would be time for the last laugh when he's begging to be picked up on my next trip here!

Ignoring the brusqueness, Dutton held out his hand in farewell. Then picking up his bag, he clambered over the rail down into the waiting dinghy. He found a place to sit on top of the sacks of mail and provisions. Shielding his eyes against the glare of the sun on the dancing waves, he tried to discern the figure in black on the waiting shore. There was also a man in white. Would that be the government doctor?

A sudden lurch of the dinghy and he forgot about those on shore. He clung with both hands to steady himself as the small craft rocked and tossed in the choppy waters. Careful, he thought, for he had heard of boats overturning here, with the more helpless drowning in the sight of all. They were getting nearer now. One wave, the second, and then a third, which, in one swelling motion, deposited the dinghy with a crunching thump on the swirling, shifting sands. "Jump," came a voice from the shore. Nimbly enough, Dutton jumped. His feet were wet and his clothes splattered, but he was at last on Molokai.

Collecting himself, he looked up to find the man in white striding towards him.

"Good morning. I am Dr. Mouritz, the medical superintendent of this settlement."

There was a hint of polite inquiry, but the hand held out was in welcome. Dutton returned the handshake.

"I am Joseph Dutton, from the United States," he offered. Turning to indicate the figure in the background, he queried,

"Is that Father Damien?"

He did not need the answer. There could be no doubt. In the swollen features under the battered, broad brimmed hat, was the man barely recognizable, whose picture he had seen. This was the indomitable Damien. What he did not know was that the priest was in the throes of the "reaction" stage peculiar to the lepromatous form of leprosy, during which the normally puffy features and elongated ears become even more swollen, with numerous small nodules covering the face, closing the eyes to mere slits, erupting around the bleeding lips. The hands and feet, during this period, are likewise affected, and the victim rages with fever as the system tries to combat the disease. Days, weeks, or even months later, the reaction period over, the nodules recede and the face takes on a more normal appearance until the next reaction sets in.

It was in this distressing state that Dutton now saw Damien. He was determined not to betray his shock. He advanced, holding out his hand to introduce himself.

"I am Joseph Dutton, come from the United States to

assist you, if you will allow me."

Damien was wary. He stepped back and regarded the stranger. From his attire, he was clearly not affluent.

"You must know," Damien warned, his voice a dry rasp of sound, "I cannot pay you."

The doctor drew closer and was about to say something. Hastily, Dutton pulled papers from his bag, passing them to the official.

"As I told the Health Office in Honolulu where I got these documents, I ask nothing for my services. I just want to help."

The doctor accepted the credentials silently. The priest, leaning on his staff, peered closely at Dutton.

"Help? Can you help? How I've longed for the day when someone would come to help, to take up my work, but . . . "

Dutton, aware that there was religious protocol, too, smiled resassuringly and proffered another paper.

"I also have a letter to you, Father, from His Excellency, the Bishop, asking you to accept me."

Damien's face suffused with happiness. He slowly extended his hand. Dutton clasped it firmly and they shook hands, solemnly and silently.

A loud crunch and a cacophony of screams, splashing, and terrified wails turned all three men to witness the beaching of the first contingent of new exiles for Molokai. Dr. Mouritz, realizing the uniqueness of the moment for the sick priest and his new helper, stopped Damien who instinctively had started towards his new flock. Gently restraining the tottering figure he turned him towards the waiting rig.

"Let me take care of them, this once, and you take Mr. Dutton on up to Kalawao. I am sure he must be tired after such a long journey, and you had better take care of yourself, too. Now you have someone to help you."

He laughed as he turned to the uncertain Dutton.

"I don't know whether to be happy or sorry for you! I know Father all too well. You will get little rest, that I can assure you. He would need an army to carry out all of his plans."

Damien laughed. "Yes, if I leave him in your company," he said half in jest, "you might end up discouraging him."

A young boy came up, taking Damien's arm. Dutton, bag in hand, followed. Was this handsome boy, bearing no marks of leprosy, a victim, too? He noticed that only the hands seemd affected, apparently stiffened to the appearance of claws. He was to learn later, that this was the neural form of leprosy, a semi-paralysis affecting the extremities, even the eyelids, leading to blindness unless steps are taken to keep the eyes moist.

The boy obviously adored the priest. His eyes were alive with excited but unspoken questions.

"This is my dear friend and companion," Damien said, introducing him to Dutton. "I don't know how I would manage without Himano."

Nodding to Dutton, he then introduced the stranger to the boy.

"This is Brother Joseph, who has come to live with us."

Dutton, startled at hearing himself called Brother, decided not to disclaim it. That could wait, he thought.

III

They had been clip-clopping along for some time now. Daisy, the tired old horse, seemed to need little guidance. Her ears protruded from the old straw hat, her tail flailing from right to left, switching at the stinging green flies lighting on her white flanks. There were only occasional breaks in the companionable silence that engulfed both men as the blazing sun beat down on them.

Clip-clop, clip-clop. Like the swinging of the metronome, ticking off the moments between yesterday and tomorrow! A sense of prelude.

Himano broke the silence.

"This is called the Father Damien Road," he proclaimed proudly. "It was Father who built this so that we could better bring in the new *mai pake*."

Damien roused himself. "He means the sick ones."

"When I first arrived," Damien added, "We had to go by foot over the mountain. There was no road. At first I cut out a path—but in the wet season it was slick mud, and crusty deep furrows in the dry. Fortunately I was able to get the more able-bodied men to help me build a road, once they saw I was determined to make it by myself, if needs be."

He lapsed into silence, his mind already full of possibilities, now that here was the promise of a full-fledged helper. This man seemed able and willing, which was more than he could say about others who had come and gone.

"Doctor Mouritz," Dutton ventured. "He seems like a very nice man. Do you work together?"

The priest smiled to himself, at some private memory. Should he level with this man or wait and let him find out things for himself? He grunted.

"You may as well know from the start. I'm not an easy man to get along with. When I first came here, there was no one. I had to do as best I could with the few simple remedies I had brought along. My poor people didn't trust anyone but me, and I must confess, I had small reason to trust anyone sent by the government. Doctor

Mouritz had heard many tales before he came so I guess he was prepared for rebellion on my part. It took a little while, but we finally got together. He had what I couldn't supply and, after all, that's what I was here for, to help my poor people, not to keep aid from them. So I did what I could to convince them to let the doctor help. Eventually he realized too, that we both wanted the same thing—to help. So now we have become friendly. He is a good man," he added, with conviction.

There seemed nothing more to say. Damien lapsed into silence and Dutton was alone with his thoughts. He had heard that Damien was difficult and to expect the worst. He had not expected that this bear-like man would speak so frankly and humbly of his faults.

The jungle-like growth on either side of the road had given way to signs of habitation. Neat cottages and the beginnings of new buildings appeared. Clumps of smiling people waved as they drove by. Some were on crutches, some blind. He noted with surprise that he was already accustomed to the signs of affliction to the point that he was seeing the onlookers not as cases of leprosy but as interesting people similar to those he had observed on the streets of Honolulu.

Damien had roused himself to greet his friends. He accepted their marks of love and respect, raising his swollen hands in acknowledgment. Occasionally he made the sign of the cross over them in blessing. He turned to Dutton.

"Did you know that my name was once Joseph?"

Dutton had read only of "Father Damien"—it had not crossed his mind as to what the priest's Christian name would be. But Joseph! A coincidence, certainly, but to him a sign, too, that God's Providence ruled all things sweetly.

"My name wasn't always Joseph," Dutton hastened to

explain. "My name was Ira, but I took the name of Joseph when I was baptized a few years ago."

"Oh?"

The priest turned to look at Dutton.

"Then you weren't born in the Catholic faith?"

"No, Father, my parents were Anglicans of a sort. At one time I had considered joining the Anglican priesthood. Then, after my conversion to Catholicism, I spent some time with the Trappists, trying to find where God wants me. But . . . " and his voice trailed off. "It's a long story, Father . . . "

Damien interrupted understandingly.

"I don't want to pry," he said. "We all have a story to tell." Turning to the original subject, he added, "I was Joseph until I joined my brother, Pamphile, at the seminary in Louvain. I took the name of Damien, the brave physician of Cilicia who spent his lifetime in the service of others, dying the death of a martyr."

For the second time during that long ride, Dutton was struck by the simplicity of the man who had described himself without realizing it. And he wondered again at the workings of Divine Providence which, even in the simple choice of names, somehow showed the inscrutable hand of God.

IV

He was alone at last. The afternoon had seemed interminable. They had arrived at Kalawao when the sun was at its blazing peak, not the best time to judge anything. There had been those quiet moments in Damien's church, though, which helped to put things in perspective. He had been warned that Damien was a careless, slovenly man. Stepping into the church and assailed by the fragrance of blossoms, he had marveled at the exquisite cleanliness of the place. Everything bespoke the handiwork of a man who not only revered God but loved beauty, balance and orderliness. The brass candlesticks gleamed, the linens were crisp and snowy white. This was not put out just for him, he knew, for no one had been expecting him.

At his entrance, an old woman, on her hands and knees industriously plying a coconut husk and bits of tallow to bring the floor to a rich sheen, arose and tiptoed out, leaving him to savor the moment alone. There was a pervasive smell of incense. He closed his eyes, his soul caught up in a deep peace. Thousands of watery miles from his homeland, yet never had he felt so much at home. He opened his eyes to see the sun's rays resting on the golden Tabernacle door. He closed his eyes again. He was closer than ever to Gethsemani, but even closer to God.

The transition to Damien's house was indescribable, he decided. What a man! It was apparent Damien thought nothing of himself, reserving for the church what beauty he had to offer. There was a small kitchen, an even smaller office, and a bedroom leading off from the almost bare parlor. The furniture was crude: a homemade desk, a large rotting rattan chair, two small kitchen chairs and a rough kitchen table. On the walls was a fading, fly-specked print of the Sacred Heart, and a dusty crucifix, the metal parts blackened and rusty in spots.

Plates and cups were made of hammered tin cans, but at least they were shining clean. The old woman who had been working in the church had prepared a light lunch. Hard boiled eggs, still in their shells, freshly cut pine-apple and, at his request, a glass of milk. Dutton noticed that Damien only nibbled at a hardtack biscuit, soon pushing away from the table to light his pipe. He puffed steadily for a moment or so, then laid the pipe down.

"There's the matter of where you will stay," he began. He jerked his head around and waved a hand disparagingly. "You can see I am not exactly prepared for you. You can go over to the other side of the island and stay with the government people, or," noting the shake of Dutton's head, "you can stay in the spare room upstairs. No one has occupied it for many months, and it is quite clean."

"That will be fine," Dutton responded hastily. "I would rather be closer to my work, for I can see there is much to be done, and I like to get an early start. Judging from the heat here, it's a good thing I am accustomed to rising about 4:30 a.m."

And so here he was, up in the spare room, furnished as sparsely as the quarters of his host below. It had been Damien who had suggested that he might wish to retire early. They were too new to each other for any long conversations and both needed some time alone.

The first thing he did when he closed the door was to open his bag and take out the picture of his mother. Relaxed and at peace, he stretched out on the cot and gave forth a long, contented sigh. Home, he breathed softly, home at last.

And then the memories crowded in on him, like the ceaseless, pounding waves of the nearby surf. Wave upon wave, each one bringing in a segment to leave on the shore, and then another, and yet another.

He looked at the picture of his mother, and thought of his happy, protected childhood—his mother both teacher and friend, sharing the long hours together during the frequent absences of his father supervising his scattered businesses. He had been only four years old when his parents moved from Stowe, Vermont, to Zanesville, Wisconsin, in 1847. Even now he could see those flattened mud roads called streets. He smiled as he thought of his howling protest against being sent to school, he who was reading, with his mother's tutelage, Emerson, Long-fellow, Hawthorne and Shakespeare! And then a whole new world opened up to him, the part time job in the newspaper office which led to another in the local book-store. It is only by giving up what we hold in one hand that God can fill both hands to overflowing, he realized. He had thought all was lost when he had left the peace and quiet of Gethsemani. Now here he was, in Molokai, with a chance for both solitude, penance, and a life of service!

He sat up and peered out of the open window. The sun's rays were growing long now, and it seemed it would soon be dusk. An owl sounded a querulous "whoooo" as a scarlet bird, with shadings of blue and black, outlined with yellow, pertly regarded him from the gently moving branch of a nearby tree. What did it make him think of? And as it came back to him he laughed aloud. He must have looked something like that when he first donned the uniform of the local Zouaves! All brilliant plumage and full of confidence! He, and the others like him, proudly strutting, confident that if war was declared, they would be ready.

And the war came, he thought grimly, and the little tinsel soldiers, now in the drab blue of the Union, came face to face with mud and cold, with real bullets and death. He shivered at the memory and laid back on the bed. War is hell, he decided, even a righteous war. And let's not think of hell in this beautiful paradise of nature.

He was motionless for a while, willing himself not to think. He wondered whatever happened to the girl who had slipped him her picture and kissed him goodbye as he had boarded the train which was to carry him and his contingent to camp. He had carried that picture for years. Whatever happened to it? It was an innocent, purely romantic thing of dreams, a bloodless emotion born of a patriotic fervor. He didn't even know her name. She was pure and a dream to worship from afar. Certainly she was not Eloise.

Eloise! The memory of her arose unbidden. Almost against his will, the memory of the first time he had seen her crowded into his consciousness. He had been so war weary that night he had gone into Nashville. That day he had been cutting off supply lines of a gallant, outnumbered enemy, blasting bridges. That night he had felt like a blast of his own. He had gone to the most likely place for excitement and diversion, not expecting much more than a brief dalliance at most. Those Southern belles had a way with them, he remembered, as if explaining to himself what came next.

He and Jeb Holden, his company clerk, had paired off early with two vivacious young women whose chaperones kept them under watchful eye. The only thing he could recall was their constant chatter. He had absented himself a couple of times for a hasty swig behind a potted palm. Lord, he had thought, I would have done better to have stayed at camp and worked on my report.

My life might have had a different ending if I had. He shook his head at the thought. For it was on the next sally onto the crowded floor, during a lively Virginia Reel that she had danced by, a dazzlingly beautiful girl in billowing yellow satin, blonde curls gleaming in the candlelight. Even now his scalp tingled as he remembered the brief, overpowering moment when their eyes met.

She had been so lovely, every line of her promising and exciting—the creamy white shoulders, the smooth rounded bosom, the dainty figure, all grace and allure. He couldn't take his eyes off her and wondered how he could manage an introduction. The music stopped, and in the interlude he abandoned his fluttering companion to seek out the girl in yellow, pushing his way through to the center of clamoring admirers asking for the next dance. Obviously she was known to many. Nor did there seem to be any uneasy chaperone hovering in the background. She had looked him up and down, from his broad shoulders down to his polished boots, seemingly pleased by what she saw. He was clean shaven at the time, and hoped his mere twenty-two years would not have her thinking he was only a callow youth. She smiled, then, and emboldened, he had caught her hand, raising it to his lips. She had that little trick of cocking her head to one side, a habit with her, he remembered. She had looked up into his eyes coquettishly, swaying a little with the music which had just struck up with a waltz. With her unspoken assent, he had put his arm around her waist—how small a waist it was! He had been enamoured from the start. His hands had passed along the satin folds of her dress, the sensuous smell of the gardenia in her hair adding its intoxication. He was strangely stirred and wished the dance would go on forever.

He shifted position in his bed and winced at the remembrance of what followed.

They had danced and danced. He could not let her go. If they stayed any longer others would come and claim her. Tentatively he had suggested a walk outside, feeling much in need of air. She had not seemed to mind, apparently even expected it. They had found a secluded spot and he had gallantly taken off his coat to spread it on the ground as a seat for her. It was quiet out there, the music a faint echo in the distance. She had smiled up at him, her fan waving her flushed cheeks.

"I don't even know your name," she had laughed, teasingly. "I'm Eloise, Eloise Headington. And you?"

"I'm Ira," he had responded, dropping down beside her. "Lt. Ira B. Dutton, Sergeant Quartermaster, stationed for the moment in Decatur."

He hoped she would not realize that his duties were behind the lines, not on the battlefield, realizing that he wanted to impress this desirable creature, to hold her again in his arms. He leaned over to her, not daring or even knowing how to put into words the longing welling up inside him. The moon had come out from behind a cloud, shining on her glistening shoulders, bringing into relief the twin roundness swelling so enticingly just below.

"Eloise!" He breathed it softly. "Eloise. What a beautiful name! And how beautiful you are!" She fluttered her fan, her lips parted invitingly. He could resist it no longer. He had pulled her to him, his lips covering hers. She had melted in his arms, returning his kiss eagerly. They had clung together, wordlessly. He could feel the warmness of her through his shirt. The music was lost in the pounding of their hearts, nor did she resist as his fingers passed caressingly over the satiny skin, down the trim bodice, exploring, then fumbling with the ribbons that tied her waist. The gardenia in her hair fell to the ground as they crushed in a savage embrace, the war forgotten, all restraints forgotten, in the intoxicating magic of that moment.

Afterwards, ashamed and repentant, he could only gaze at the stemless broken flower, already browning at his feet. Yet ashamed as he was, he could not resist extracting her promise to meet with him again. And again, and again, he remembered.

He rose from his cot to pace the floor. Will I ever get her out of my blood, he wondered. He had not been the first, that he knew, for his friends had tried to warn him when they saw his involvement. Yet he had somehow felt a sense of responsibility. She was originally from a small town in Indiana, he had learned.

The infatuation had passed and he had recognized it for what it was. He did not love her, nor she him, yet she had awakened in him many and mixed emotions and needs. Mostly he had wanted to rescue her from her associates. Perhaps all she needed was a new start, away from the fast and loose company of wartime revelries. And always there was the thought of how soft and yielding she was, how exciting, yes, even how wanton she could be. Eloise, Eloise! How I longed to save you, but you would not. Even the respectability of marriage had not done that.

He had sent her to live with some friends of his in Alabama, then later to Mount Vernon in Ohio, until he was free to do something about their relationship. There they had been married, on New Year's Day, 1866. It was to be a new beginning, they had promsied each other. Yet, in less than a year she was gone. There had come another man who had promised, not respectability, but excitement. She was like a butterfly, flitting from flower to flower. The last he had heard of her, following the uncontested divorce, was that she had died in New York, abandoned and penniless.

He stared moodily out of the window. The roaring ocean pulsing out there against the unyielding rocks was in harmony with the throbbing in his head. Poor, broken butterfly!

Restlessly he returned to the cot and stretched out, hands under his head. He hoped that his weariness would take over and that sleep would put an end to these unwanted, painful memories.

There were those long, sleepless nights that had followed Eloise's flight. With a fresh sense of shame he remembered his turning more and more to alcohol to drown out his disillusionment and betrayal—his sense of failure really, he amended the thought. Five long years of secret debauchery and self-debasement, his days were crammed with work, his nights filled with drunken despair.

He was no better than she, he acknowledged humbly. She had had her weakness and he certainly had his. Now it was all over. For good or for bad, leave it to God. What remained was to do penance for his sins. He had thought Gethsemani held the answer. He had tried, for twenty long months, to succeed at least in this. Hours of prayer balanced with hours of good hard work in the fields, and always the blessed silence. It was penance, yes, but not the penance he sought. It was too self-centered, too turned back onto self. He needed something harder, something outside himself, something constructive, with daily goals. He wanted, not to leave people, but to love them, to serve them. And if they were people whom no one else loved, so much the better.

Here, on Molokai, he would do his penance, among these suffering, afflicted ones bearing the marks of the Sinless One. Indeed, he thought, *with* the Sinless One, atoning in their ravaged bodies for the sins of a heedless world.

He felt for his crucifix and, in the dark, pressed it to his lips. For me, dear Lord, for me? God had guided him to this day, this place. In God he would find his strength.

The steady wash of the surf was having a hypnotic effect. He found himself counting the waves—one—two— jump on the third, he remembered. He could see the swirling waters when he had jumped—was it only this morning? One—two—he wondered what was the reason for waiting for the third wave to jump. He would have to inquire about that, he promised himself dreamily. One— two—he did not reach the third.

Book Two

———••••———

With Damien:
A Life Shared

I

For Damien it had been a sleepless night. He had not come to any conclusions about this new helper of his. He seemed promising enough, and Lord knows he needed him.

But there had been the others. Some who stayed only a month or so; others who, hanging on for a year or two, spent most of their time writing to the Bishop with all sorts of stories. It was a relief when they left. There was something about this new one, though, that was strangely reassuring.

Obviously he respected authority. He had gone through all the proper channels. And he was devout, going straight to the church the first chance he had. A convert, he said he was. But . . . a passing fervor, perhaps?

Yet there was that quiet determination, the straight and unwavering gaze. And the man had muscles! There was a dignity about him, too, a quiet, somewhat humble assurance. Damien turned painfully on his bed. Oh, God, he groaned, let this one work out. Time is getting short, don't forget, he reminded the Lord, familiarly. He turned again, fingering the soiled coverlet. Perhaps he should get up right now and outline some plans he had been revolving in his mind that afternoon. The thought of lighting the lamp deterred him, however. He pulled up the coverlet and turned over again.

Dutton was a young forty, he decided. He seemed quite interested in the children. Perhaps this was the time to try to start a school, for the boys, at least. If the Sisters ever came, they could take over the girls. Well, we shall see what we shall see. And with this bit of peasant wisdom, he took up his rosary and counted, rather than prayed, the hours to dawn.

II

He was on a battlefield. Mist was swirling over rotting stumps and disjointed, crumbling walls. Somehow his mother was there, too, searching with him, for what it wasn't clear. Somewhere in the distance a rooster crowed. It crowed again, nearer this time. Dutton sat up with a jerk. It was already sunrise! How could he have overslept, on this, his very first morning at Molokai!

He had slept the night through, still in his clothes. He had only to slip on his canvas slippers and run his fingers through his curling locks. He emerged on the porch to a beauty that was ever to amaze him. The lush growth gave off an almost overpowering sweetness, mixed with the scent of burnt-out fires and the tangy salt of the ceaselessly pounding surf. The steep cliffs were a soft blue in the morning haze. There were gently swaying, rustling palms, purple bougainvillea and deep-scented frangipanni, trees of velvety green with brilliant red blossoms. Nearby the rooster crowed once more, then ceased, satisfied that it had properly saluted this new day.

He could not stop to drink it all in. He only hoped he had not missed Mass. He hurried anxiously to the church. On his entrance, he was surprised and deeply moved to find Damien and the congregation patiently waiting for him. Damien motioned for him to come to the sacristy.

"Good morning, Brother Joseph," he twitted the discomforted, apologetic Dutton. "I trust you slept well?" The priest's head emerged from the alb he was donning. "Don't apologize . . . you've had a long voyage and it is going to take you a few days to get adjusted."

With a reassuring smile at Himano who was holding his chasuble, Damien looked at Dutton.

"Would you serve my Mass? Himano won't mind this time, I'm sure. It will be good for my people to know that here is a white man who shares their religion."

"It would be a privilege and an honor, Father." Dutton could not contain his joy. He had expected, when he had left the cloister, never again to function within the sanctuary. Himano preceding, the two men approached the altar. Mass went slowly, with Damien moving unsteadily.

The moment of Communion came and Dutton knelt to receive the Host from Damien's hand. The poignancy of the moment was lost, however, in the commotion that followed a veritable wave of people towards the rail. Accustomed as he was to the infrequent Communions in the States, it seemed to him that the entire congregation would be receiving. He held the paten as Damien placed the Host on each tongue. What a moment of almost palpable, all-embracing love! Each communicant, in one way or another, bore the mark of the suffering Christ. The simplicity and starkness of their faith was an experience he would never forget, he thought, even if the Lord spared him for fifty years. He felt more at home here than he ever had in the Kentucky cloister.

During the thanksgiving that followed the Mass, while Damien prayed before his crucifix, Dutton returned to the altar. Kneeling there, in the silence of his heart, he made his first but perpetual vows: Poverty, yes! He was already poor. Chastity, too! Of that he was determined. Obedience he could manage, he was sure. But, most of all, stability. Here he was, and here he would stay! He would leave, never!

III

Doctor Mouritz was waiting for them when they came out of the church. The people were grouped outside, anxious to see more closely this stranger described by Himano. Some had fashioned leis which they placed in welcome around Dutton's neck. Mouritz smiled. Evidently Mr. Dutton had survived the night with no misgivings. So far, so good.

Father Damien held up his hand for silence.

"This is Brother Dutton," he announced. "He has come from far away to help us. Anything he asks you to do, it is I who have told him to do it. Now begone, and let us have some breakfast. It is late already."

"Come on up to the house, Doctor," he invited. "There's much to talk about. And I suppose you have a report on our new sick ones, eh?"

The three men walked slowly towards the house. Inside, the doctor stood to one side as Damien and Dutton blessed themselves and broke bread. Dutton looked inquiringly up at the doctor, and Damien laughed.

"Oh, he's had breakfast already, I know. Hours ago! How were the eggs I sent over yesterday?"

"Excellent, as usual. If we could depend on our other supplies as we can depend on your chickens, wouldn't it be wonderful." And both men laughed at some joke they shared between them. Mouritz regarded Dutton.

"You'll get used to very early rising here," he proffered. "We have to get most of our work done before the noonday heat."

Dutton almost blurted out that he was more than used to early hours, in the cold, unrelieved gray mornings of Kentucky's Gethsemani, but caught himself. This was a part of his life that only he and Damien would know.

It was Damien who broke the awkward silence.

"I could hardly sleep last night, thinking of all the things we can now get done. I hardly know where to start with you, Brother." He looked from Dutton to Mouritz. The doctor rose to the bait.

"We could use some help at the dispensary if you would like to start there?"

Aware of the implied challenge, Dutton drained his glass of milk before replying, glancing at Damien. The doctor mistook the look.

"That is, if you're willing, of course. It wouldn't take long to teach you the modicum medical skills needed!"

Dutton swallowed hastily.

"Why, fine, Doctor! You see I already have some general medical experience from my stint in the Civil War, simple bandaging and the like. The war between the States," he hastened to add, aware that Hawaii was far removed from what had transpired in far off America.

"A former soldier!"

The doctor beamed. That accounted for the erect stance he had noted yesterday, the squared shoulders, that free, swinging gait. The clothes were faded and worn, but the man was neat and clean. There was a certain discipline here, he decided. This was getting better and better. He leaned forward with heightened interest.

Dutton mentally kicked himself. He had not intended to get into these details, at least not so soon. But he could not ignore the interest his statement had generated. He downplayed it, as best he could, briefly explaining that he had been with the quartermaster corps which mostly involved supplies and materiel, and, of course, much bookkeeping. He did not notice the look that passed between Damien and Mouritz.

Damien picked up the word "bookkeeping." For the first time in many a moon he threw back his head and laughed aloud. The doctor joined in. Dutton looked in puzzlement, first at Damien, then at Mouritz, and then back at Damien. He didn't catch the joke.

"Bookkeeping," Damien gasped, and the laughter started all over again.

Damien was the first to recover, apologizing for not being able to include Dutton in their glee.

"Bookkeeping," he sputtered, dabbing at his eyes, "Bookkeeping! At last, someone to unscramble my books!" He flashed an impish look at Mouritz whose eyes were still bright with merriment. "Won't the Board of Health be happy when they get a report that they can finally decipher!"

IV

Damien was feeding his chickens. Dutton, watching from the verandah, could not take his eyes from the homely scene. Was this the officious, overbearing, ruthless Damien he had been warned to expect!

There the man was, barely able to stand, tossing the

feed first to one side, then the other. He was clucking to them happily, even talking to them it seemed. The chickens were everywhere, running over his feet, one perched precariously on his shoulder, flapping its wings for balance and squawking. Damien raised his hand with seed just for her. Dutton heard the name, Gretchen. This must be his pet, he thought. It was a gentle Damien he saw, a lonely man among his friends. It was a side of Damien his critics could not see. Christ, Who railed at Pharisees, and, with knotted cord, drove the money changers from the temple, could also melt with tenderness to cry out, "Jerusalem, Jerusalem, how I have longed to save you, as a mother hen would her chicks." It was the same with Damien, he decided. The gruffness and belligerence was for those who would neglect the needs of his people, like the angry goose he remembered who flailed at him with her wings when, as a child, he had attempted to pick up her gosling.

Damien, unaware of an audience, scattered the last of the feed far out so that the more timid ones on the fringe could get it. He leaned over in evident pain, picked up his staff and slowly straightened, brushing at his stained cassock. Leaving the chickens still pecking industriously at what was left, he carefully locked the gate and started towards the house. Dutton withdrew hastily. He had a feeling that this was a private side of the man best left with Damien.

V

The day was passing quickly enough. After breakfast, the doctor had taken Dutton to the infirmary, all business now. The able-bodied had assembled for medicines for their assorted ailments. There's more here than leprosy, the doctor reminded him. They have their stomach-aches like anyone else, especially when they've had too much *poi*.

He noticed that not once had the doctor actually touched a single hand.

"Who does the bandaging now?" he inquired.

"They like to take care of themselves when they can. The very sick are another matter. Damien has been the one, for all these years, but lately has tried to train one of the young men."

The doctor was somewhat stiff and evasive, Dutton noticed, but felt he had to push the point.

"Then there's not that much in actually taking care of their sores!"

"Oh, there's always plenty of that to be done, even with help. You haven't seen the really bad cases," the doctor warned, "but don't worry, Father Damien still insists on reserving those for himself."

Dutton wondered if the momentary expression that flitted across the doctor's face was one of relief or an inward shame. Perhaps a little of both, he decided, not blaming the man. Professional dedication is one thing, but there are limits to even clinical detachment. Damien was there, where and when love was needed, he thought. He remembered some of the cases of gangrene among the wounded brought back from the battlefield into his camp, and of his own instinctive reaction at the time. But now he was ready for it. Penance was never meant to be easy. He would have to speak to Father tonight about lightening his load. He must not allow himself ever to forget why he was here.

If the doctor had thought to shock the newcomer by taking him to the bedside of one man in a particularly bad case of reaction, he was instead, surprised and impressed. Looking at the invalid, Dutton recalled to mind a Biblical prophecy: "A Man scorned and reviled—there is no wholeness in Him." This victim was covered with corrupting flesh, literally with no spot that could be called whole. Dutton, not realizing that the imminence of death would bring its own spontaneous apparent "healing" process, wondered how the poor priest could find a spot for anointing. His compassion blotted out all aversion. He leaned over the man to take his hand, inquiring if there was anything he could do for him.

The doctor coughed. "Come, Brother," he cautioned, "we'll tell Father Damien that Tamasoa needs him. I'll bring him over first thing tomorrow morning," he reassured the man, as Dutton lingered to comfort him. Good Lord! the doctor thought. Obviously this man had no care for his personal safety. He wondered if, in a few years, there would be another martyr on Molokai.

The tour was detailed and Dutton tried to absorb it all, especially the various treatments that had been tried and some they were considering. There was talk of Curgun oil, he was told, which was in use in India and seemed to have promise, but word had it that it was difficult to administer.

"Then there's talk of a special remedy called the 'Goto method,' devised by a Japanese doctor which is now being tried with patients at Kakaako," Mouritz explained. "Damien himself has tried it—a combination of diet, medication and hot baths, and is quite enthusiastic. He'll probably talk to you about it before long, as he wants to construct a bath center here."

During the tour, from the infirmary to the houses of the sufferers, the children were underfoot everywhere. Children with faces of old people, children with hardly a mark on them, children with features swollen and blotched with festering sores, played as children will play, impish and mischievous, oblivious of tragedy and death. Darting in and out, they somehow managed always to be in front of Dutton, as if intent on judging this man for themselves.

"Have you ever played hopscotch?"

"Opascot?"

Dutton leaned over and drew the lines he remembered from his childhood. Then, picking up a stone he threw it into the first square, agilely hopping, turning, never touching a line. They laughed in delight, then tried it, awkwardly enough at first, howling in derision when one fell in the dust. Picking up another stone, Dutton threw it into the second, then the third square, turning and skipping back, the children following suit. They caught on surprisingly fast. They are smart enough he thought. What a pity that they didn't have a school. Another mental memo for Damien.

It was with a shrieking, laughing pack in tow that he arrived back at the house. The children rushed to Damien, who was sitting on the porch with his breviary, telling him with flourishes and swirling interpretation, all about "opascot."

Damien smiled fondly at their eager, excited faces, and closed the book. He had still to end his Vespers, but it could wait.

"Away with you, and give Brother some peace," Damien chided. But there was no hint of scolding in his voice. He gazed speculatively at Dutton. If only this man lasted!

VI

After the evening meal they sat out on the porch in silence, Damien puffing on his pipe. It had been a long day for the priest, too, struggling with the maze of "records" still unrecorded, trying to put some sense into his hurried scribblings, so that he could turn over this onerous task to Dutton.

The heat was intense, but a breeze was blowing in from the ocean. The air was sweet, and the strange cluckings and warblings of the birds mingled with the ceaseless roar of the surf. It was a peaceful, satisfying moment, with each man deep in his own thoughts.

Dutton was the first to break the silence.

"I saw a great deal today, Father," he began, describing his tour and ending with an account of Tamasoa's condition. "As a priest you can do for him what no one else can. But if you would not mind, I would like to help you with whatever else has to be done for him. And the others like him," he added.

"I won't pretend it will be easy for me," he continued. "But then, that's one of the reasons I am here. To help you, yes, but also to do penance."

He looked at Damien. Should he tell him everything? Or should he await another time, after he had proven himself?

"You must know, Father," he began, clearing his throat, "that my life has not been exemplary. When I tell you everything, you may not want me to stay. But I will have to take that chance, because you have the right to know me for what I am."

Damien took his pipe from his mouth, to look more closely at the quiet figure half sitting, half leaning against the post. The hands were trembling, he noted, but the gaze was direct and unflinching.

"Please, Brother, do not distress yourself. There is no hurry about this. You have closed the book on all that went before, I am sure. There is no one, least of all myself, with any right to know anything, except that you want to serve God and his afflicted. God knows, my friend, and that is all that matters."

"Well, Father, I appreciate that, but I think I want to open that book this once, if only to reassure you that God has led me here and here I intend to stay, as long as you will allow me. I want to lay the ground for perfect trust, Father, and this means you have to really know me. . . ."

He paused, pondering his approach.

"I am not an idle visionary, as some have undoubtedly judged, nor is this some passing fervor which will vanish with the rising sun. I have sinned grievously, against God, against others, and against myself. For this I am determined to do penance."

Damien interrupted, consolingly, "Sometimes we think we are the worst of sinners, until we come up with real evil, and then we know the difference!" As Dutton shook his head in disclaimer the priest acquiesced. "Well, have it your way," he said, gently. "Tell me about it."

Dutton paused in thought, groping for the right words. It was one thing to want to pour out his soul, to seek peace in true understanding as well as in sacramental pardon. But where did one really begin?

"It's not a pretty picture, Father," he began, "but don't think I'm despondent, I know God has forgiven me, and that is why I want to give Him something in return. I don't even despair over the episodes of my life, tragic as some were, and dissolute, too, for years. Everything has its purpose in the plans of God, even our weaknesses. I really believe this."

Damien leaned forward, his pipe forgotten. He regarded the serious face before him. The conviction, the earnestness, the controlled movements were not part of his picture of dissoluteness as he had viewed it. If anything, this man seemed to possess a self discipline which he himself had never attained.

"You say you have offended God." He laid down his now cold pipe. "We all have offended God, and continue to offend Him, though seldom with malice, which is where the real evil is. And I daresay we will continue to offend God until our dying day. But God knows the heart and He has a very special clause of mercy for us who aspire to mountain climbing, only to end up in daily little ruts. In His good time He will accomplish in us what we can never do of ourselves."

"Yes, Father, I believe that. But there have been sins against others . . ." His voice trailed off. How could he explain Eloise to this priest? The sins, yes, and Lord knows he had done penance for them, before and after the ill-fated marriage. Was the sense of unfinished business due, not so much to his failure with Eloise as his betraying the trust and upbringing of his devoted mother?

"My mother," he began, and a happy thought struck him. "Just a minute, Father, I have a picture I would like to show you." And he hurried upstairs, coming down with his mother's picture which he handed over to Damien.

Damien peered closely at the features of the gentle-faced woman, seeing in his mind's eye his own beloved mother.

"All children fail their parents in one way or another, in some cases in many ways," he remarked, tactfully. He looked into Dutton's eyes, trying to soften the moment of self-revelation.

"Have you heard that wise observation?" He quoted: "Children when they are young step on your feet; when they grow up they step on your heart!" He blinked at a painful thought. "The last sorrow I caused my mother was not of my doing, however. I had tried to keep from her the news of my illness, but somehow word got to her that her 'brave Joseph' was an outcast, afflicted with a vile disease. It killed her, as surely as if they had plunged a knife in her heart." Then, noting Dutton's sympathy, he urged, "But go on, and tell me about your mother. Is she still living?"

Dutton shook his head, mutely. He reclaimed the picture, gazing at it soberly. God had spared her much of the sordid episodes of his life. At least, she did not die with heartbreak, having followed him into the Church before her death. But there was the wrench of his childhood years and the break that had first come into her life when he was taken from her. He tried to explain some of this to Damien.

Damien, the product of the Old World where villages counted their history by centuries, found it hard to visualize the bustling small towns springing up like mushrooms throughout the expanding New World pushing its frontiers from the Atlantic across the continent to the Pacific.

Dutton described his precocious childhood as the only companion to his pretty young mother during his father's long absences. He explained his passion for books and how, reluctant as he was to enroll for formal education, soon forgot his mother's new loneliness in the life opened up to him by the part time jobs in the bookstore and the printing shop which took him more and more away from her side.

"You are right, Father," he said, "we do indeed walk over the hearts of our parents. I can still see the stricken look on my mother's face as I forgot everything at the sight of all those books in the headmaster's office, hardly saying goodbye as she turned and went back home alone."

"Yes," replied Damien, "I did that to my people, too. You see, my father had already given one son to the priesthood and he had banked on me to carry on his work as a merchant. But I was determined, even though I had not had the proper scholastic beginning—nothing else mattered to me but that I be a Religious like my brother. It was a big disappointment to both my father and mother. And then, when I volunteered to leave Belgium, writing them while en route to these far-off islands, where they would never see me again, they were the ones making the sacrifice. I was following my call . . . "

"It was something like that with me," reminisced Dutton, struck by the similarities. "I had secretly joined the Zouaves, preparing for the war which I could see shaping up. My parents only knew about it as I got notice to leave for mobilization camp. I was so proud of myself, my uniform, I barely gave heed to the suffering I was inflicting on those I left at home."

Damien picked up his pipe, relit it and puffed at it in silence. Dutton placed the picture of his mother carefully on the rail, and sat down on the step, looking up at Damien.

"There was a girl, Father. Even now I can't quite explain what my motives were in marrying her. I seemed to forget all my early upbringing, the teachings of my mother and my church. Nothing mattered but Eloise. Something in her brought out the worst in me. I guess remorse took over and I tried to right a wrong, or maybe, for once, I was thinking of someone other than myself and thought I could save her. I don't know. I only know she was like an addiction, just as much as the bouts with the bottle after she left me. There wasn't much difference, really. She could inflame me like the strongest liquor, making me forget everything. And then I would awaken to shame and self-recrimination, only to live for the next evening and the intoxication she brought. After she left, the liquor sufficed. Five long years of evil companions and self-indulgence! I could get my work done each day, but the nights! You wouldn't know the transformation. It was as if there were two of me. But the time came, finally, when I realized I had to 'cast out the devil' as it were. Perhaps it was my mother's prayers, like Monica's for Augustine. But God gave me the grace to turn my back on it all. And ever since I have been a pilgrim, seeking to make amends to God. My pilgrimage has led me to my new Faith, and on to the Trappists' cloister, and now to Molokai. I believe God has brought me here, and here, with God's grace, I will stay."

Damien's pipe had grown cold again. He tapped it out.

"God has indeed worked in your soul, Brother," he assured him. "And your coming is a balm for my own soul. I will have you in mind as I finish my breviary. Rest well, for I have many plans for tomorrow."

Alone with his breviary, Damien took up his interrupted Vespers. "Nunc dimitis," he read, "Now Thou dost dismiss Thy servant, O Lord . . . " Quietly he closed the book. Two hearts were at peace . . .

VII

"You seem to have a way with children. What would you think of the idea of starting a school for them?"

The two men were finishing their breakfast of eggs, hardtack and coffee. Damien, his eyes on Dutton, waited to see what Dutton's reaction would be. Would he be like the others who at one time or another had come, only to follow their own bent with their own ideas of what they wanted to do.

For his part, Dutton was delighted that the idea was coming from Damien, without any suggestion from him.

"Father," he said, "I was a military man. You are my captain. You give the orders and I will do it. I may get an idea or two and I hope to be free to discuss it with you, but you are the one to decide. I have come to help you wherever you can use me."

Damien could not hide his satisfaction.

"Splendid," he exclaimed, pounding the table and pushing back his chair. This man was willing to follow, to see service not in just bandaging sores but in caring for larger, more basic needs of those at Molokai.

"Look here. This is my plan," and he pulled out from the sleeve of his cassock a crumpled paper which he pushed over to Dutton.

Together they mulled over the crude sketch, Dutton sharing the excitement of Damien. Together they walked out to where Damien thought they might be able to construct a modest, one-room schoolhouse of sorts.

"One thing, though, Brother," Damien sighed, "it's going to take some time. I wish we could start on this right away, but I'm not as strong as I used to be," and he looked at his swollen hands ruefully.

"I can be of help there, Father. You draw the plans and I will build. I am somewhat versed in carpentry. I had to build bridges as well as destroy them during the war. It will be good to put this skill to use in God's work."

Damien could not believe his good fortune. New strength seemed to pour into him. He would live! Together, he the architect and Dutton, the builder, would finish his master plan for Molokai!

"God has surely sent you to me, Brother," he exclaimed. "Let me tell you all the things that need to be done. The church, for one thing, is badly in need of repairs, perhaps even restructuring. And there's the question of a place for you. You should have your own quarters. And I would so like to build a new treatment center, install the baths for the Goto treatment. Did Dr. Mouritz mention that? But of course, the school comes first! The children have been such a worry for me."

They retraced their steps back to the house, and sitting on the verandah, they discussed how best to start the school project.

"When I first came here," the priest explained, "the plight of the children was miserable. They were abandoned, used or abused by the lusts of the adults in a most revolting fashion. I managed to gather them together for their own protection, but now they really need firm guidance. I've been begging for some Sisters for the girls, the Franciscans at the hospital in Honolulu, who have offered to come but I'm afraid I will be long gone before the Bishop gives his approval. As for the boys, since I have been sick, they have been getting out of hand. Rough as I am, when it comes to the children, I am afraid I am too indulgent. I will give you full charge of them. They may resist at first, when they realize it is not all games. Be prepared, too, for mistrust, for they have little reason to trust a white man. It was the white man who consigned them here and who keeps them here. Indeed, it was the white man's coming to Hawaii that opened the trade with the Orient which eventually brought leprosy into these peaceful islands."

"Well," said Dutton, "we will begin with what you have brought into their lives, Father. They love you and they trust you . . . "

"And that is more than I can say for anybody else," Damien said cryptically. He did not elaborate.

VIII

It was good to be using his hands again. It was good to awaken in the morning with work cut out for him to do, to be teaching, building, planning. It was exciting to have his own private quarters, a peaceful oasis in a day crammed with Damien's projects. It was even good to have more to do than he could really manage, knowing that the day would come, eventually, when he could perhaps catch up with Damien's enthusiastic demands. They worked together perfectly yet were so different. Damien brusque, tempestuous, stubborn; Dutton courteous, patient and serene.

"Please forgive me," Damien had said abruptly once. "I do not have the best of manners. I lose my temper, but it is because I am so anxious to get things done and it is so frustrating not to be able to do them myself as I once did. How I rejoiced in my strength in those days!"

Dutton had laughed.

"Don't worry about it, Father, I understand. If I could

stand the rigors of the monastery and its crusty Abbot, it is like working with angels now. Oh, he was kind," he had added hastily, "and under your rough exterior, so are you!"

Damien fidgeted uncomfortably, but Dutton had continued, banteringly.

"Don't think I don't notice you with the children. They worship you."

He was browning now, from his daily work in the sun. As he turned back to his sawing, the smaller children playing with the woodshavings, the larger ones piling up the usable leftover lengths of wood, he wondered if they would ever accept him with the trust they showed in Damien.

The answer came quite unexpectedly. He had labored far into the night at his desk, perfecting the rough plans Damien had made for the new medicinal baths. As the candle flame began to dance wildly in the draft of a coming storm, he had decided it was time to extinguish it and go to bed. He was deep in slumber when he was awakened, not so much by the sound of trees thrashing wildly about in the throes of the driving winds, or the breakers battling the rocks at the foot of cliffs, as the feeling that something, someone was in the room with him. Torrential rain drummed a steady, noisy tattoo on the corrugated tin roof.

"Who's there?" he shouted over the thunder, "who's there?"

A flash of lightning, and Dutton saw the crouching figure bending over his bed. Another flash, and he recognized the frightened face of Himano.

"What is it, lad? Surely you are not afraid of the storm!"

"Oh, no, Brother!" The protest was indignant. "It's Makaio! He's gone!" Dutton pulled aside his mosquito netting and groped for his shoes.

"Makaio? Which one is Makaio?"

By this time he was up and sloshing through the water blown in through the flapping shutters.

"The new boy, Brother, the one whose mother died the day they came. We've looked everywhere but he is gone!"

"Gone? But where could he go? Why would he go?" He was confused but already had found his jacket.

"What?" he exclaimed as Himano suggested the cemetery. "Oh, that poor child!"

He reached for his lantern, lighting it with difficulty.

"Go back, Himano, get some of the older boys to help you. Spread out. We must find him. And hurry, he is such a small child, he could be swept out to sea!"

He had experienced storms before but nothing like what greeted him as he stepped out into the raging gale, to be lashed by the stinging, needle-like rain. Water was pouring down from the cliffs above, huge rocks torn loose were crashing down into the sea below. Strong as he was, he had to cling to the undergrowth, almost crawling to make any progress against the howling wind.

He groped through inky blackness, praying for another flash of lightning to get his bearings.

"Makaio!" he screamed, sobbing from anxiety and exertion. "Makaio, answer me."

He judged he must be somewhere near the cemetery. A sudden drop in the noise as the storm prepared for its next onslaught, and he heard a faint cry. Another streak of lightning and he saw him—a small, terror-stricken child, clinging at the base of a gnarled old tree. He dropped over him in protection as there was a sharp crackling split of thunder and lightning, while the ground seemed to shake under him.

"Makaio, my little one," he soothed. "Everything will be alright." He pressed the small, shivering figure to him. Cradling him under his jacket, he found his way back, easier now with the wind behind him.

The people were huddled in the church. They crowded around him, talking excitedly, Makaio smiling through his tears, the center of their attention. The storm stopped, died off, and in the silence that fell on them, he noticed them staring at his hands.

He glanced down at his fingers. They were swollen, bruised and bleeding. Looking up, he saw in their eyes a look of love and awe. Here was a white man who would give his life for them. These were Damien's hands, and here was Damien's heart.

IX

"Goodbye, Brother, off I am."

Dutton glanced up to catch the airy wave of Damien driving away. He had to laugh. Father had taken a new lease on life, despite his steadily deteriorating health. It was almost as if he were counting his days against all that remained to be done. He was everywhere at once, giving orders, directing the mixing of the mortar, leaving him with brief instructions about one project even as he was setting out to start another.

It had been a busy two years. The settlement was humming with new life, and not just because he had come. There was the priest, Conrady, who had arrived in May. Not a member of Damien's Order, but a man somewhat of Damien's temperament, it seemed, a fellow Belgian. From all accounts his life had been somewhat colorful, first in Hindustan, and then, for fifteen years in the Indian Territory in Oregon where he had been nearly scalped.

Dutton chuckled. From his contacts with the priest he could almost see why, then chided himself for being uncharitable. But even Mother Marianne and the Sisters who had at last been allowed to come and had taken the girls to Kalaupapa, did not want him for their Confessor and so yet another priest had been assigned, and then three more in quick succession. There was also the Irishman, James Sinnott, a layman who, like himself, had arrived out of nowhere and had been immediately dubbed Brother James and set to work with him on construction.

In the midst of all the comings and goings, the new projects, Damien pushed himself with ferocity and determination. But in the evenings, the day's activity over, a sadness seemed to overtake him, a hidden agitation, sometimes a bewildered anger which led him to thrash out, following immediately with a penitent apology.

"It's nothing you've done," he'd hasten to assure the patient Dutton, "but I can't explain . . . "

They had shared confidences, Dutton completely opening himself, but Damien had always held one area private—his relations with his Congregation, which were not too good, Dutton surmised, but then it was not his business, and he concluded, perhaps the priest felt that a layman could never understand the day-by-day workings of the religious life. Damien had come back, time after time, to the subject of the Trappists and how Dutton viewed them.

"I don't think I was ever really a part of the religious community," Dutton had answered, sensing Damien's reluctance to discuss his own Congregation, "even though I lived their life. I had a great deal of respect and admiration for the Episcopalian faith to the point that the subject of Holy Orders had come up while still a member of that denomination. What I was looking for in Roman Catholicism was the possibility of a more formal concept of penance, and it was this that led me eventually to the Trappists."

"I had heard that these men slept on boards and never talked," he told the priest. "And since my idea was to do penance, to close myself against the world which I considered to be an enemy to my salvation, I thought the Trappists held the answer. Of course I soon realized that I am my own worst enemy and always will be."

A thought struck him. "Actually," he had ventured, "I guess I might say that religious life, aside from the search for and service of God, is the bringing together of many such as you and I, who eventually realize that the life is not a haven from the world, or a battle against the world, but a place where sooner or later, one finds, not only the heights of God's goodness, but the depths of one's 'humanness'. The closer we get to God," he thought aloud, "the better we see ourselves as we really are. It's a good thing God loves us, for we aren't really all that lovable! Not even in the holy cloister!"

Damien's own experiences in the cloister brought a smile to his face. But he made no comment.

"I am only now beginning to realize why so few American men persevere in the Trappist monasteries," Dutton went on. "It's not the life, the austerities, for we go through much worse under more distressing circumstances in war. Few of us are true mystics, willing to await God's plan, to allow Him to work through the weaknesses and even selfishness of others to straighten our own lives. We don't like to have things 'done for us'—if there is any 'doing' we want to do it ourselves—we must be the arbiters of our own destiny!"

At this Damien nodded vigorously.

"Ahhh," he laughed. "You have hit the nail on the head. It sounds like young Damien talking. Many a hard time

I've brought on myself because I won't let things happen *to* me. Not just you Americans—it is certainly not in my nature, either, to accept things as they happen, even the things over which I have little control. I always see things as they should be, and then do everything I can to make them so, to bend facts to my will. . . . "

There was a long pause as each continued the subject in their own hearts. Obviously it was going to take much more than this to break down the priest's reserve as to matters between him and his Congregation. Dutton realized that something was coming to a head, the ominous quiet before the storm breaks. What had gone on before he arrived, he could only surmise. But obviously, some hidden cancer was gnawing at Damien's soul, just as much as leprosy was more and more encroaching on the strength of this indomitable man.

"The vultures are gathering," Damien had remarked, darkly, rising clumsily to totter unsteadily into the house.

X

Damien was waiting for him on the verandah after a particularly discouraging day. That something had been troubling him all day, there was no doubt. His friend had alternately lashed out at the workers, apologized to all around, to stomp disconsolately back to the house where he now sat, after a supper passed in moody silence.

He was slumped, weak and sickly, in the old wicker chair. His face was mottled and blotchy, pus glistening on the angry looking nodules disfiguring his face. But the eyes were alive with purpose.

"Hitch up Daisy," he ordered peremptorily. "I want to

drive along the shore."

Dutton hesitated, not at all sure that his friend had the strength to get into the rig, much less last out the bumpy trip.

"Do you think it is wise?" he began, but stopped at the look of determination and hidden torment in the priest's whole demeanor. The boil is ready to be lanced, Dutton decided, and he needs the privacy of the shore to let it all out. The relief will be good for his soul even if it is hard on his body, he concluded, and set about preparing old Daisy who looked like she, too, was barely up to the ride.

Carefully he helped Damien into the conveyance, then took the reins and gently walked the faithful animal down the rocky road to the beach. With the suddenness peculiar to the tropics, dusk was already enveloping them by the time they found a spot along the shore, awash with the restless tide, advancing, then receding, then advancing again. On the horizon a mirrored glow of red from the sinking sun flecked the purplish blue of the waters. Before long the moon would appear, to turn the darkening waters to glittering, dancing gold. A lone gull swooped low, searching for one last morsel before night closed in. It was a peaceful scene, but a lonely one, a foretoken of the darkness of the spirit before the finality of death.

Daisy stood patiently, her head drooped forward, her white flanks the one bit of brightness in the half dark of dusk. Dutton leaned against the side of the rig. He, like Daisy, could wait.

The minutes passed by. Overhead the stately cliffs stood, silent witness to the immutable forces of nature in all its agonies. There was a sudden movement of the palms and eucalyptus as a breeze blew in across the waters, and just as suddenly, Damien cleared his throat.

"There is something that I want you to do for me,

Brother," he began, his rasping voice breaking the silence.

"Anything, Father, you know that."

Damien pulled out a pencil and paper from his worn pockets, handing them down to Dutton. "It is you that I want to write down the following. Take it, every word, just as I dictate it. Every word," he repeated, "and then I will sign it."

Dutton looked around him. Nearby was a flat rock which he could use, he decided. He lit the coconut oil lamp he had brought to light the way home. In the glow from this flickering lamp, and braced against the huge, flat rock, Dutton dutifully took down the words as Damien began:

"Rev. Father J. Damien DeVeuster, Catholic priest, native of Belgium; Belgian parents; 49 years of age. All of the members of his family very strong and healthy. No taint of scrofula or syphilis. No relatives on these islands."

Damien's voice was stronger now, and he went faster, almost as if he were reading what must have been formulating in his mind for some time.

"Served as priest on the island of Hawaii from 1864 until 1873. Occasionally heard confessions of lepers; ministered to them in their cabins sometimes, but had no constant or very personal contact with them until he came here to the leper settlement in 1873, since which time, until now, his contact and association with them have been almost constant."

Dutton, who had thought Damien had intended to write his own epitaph or perhaps was preparing his Will, suddenly realized that Damien was attempting to lay down the history of his disease as a prelude to something. *"In 1873,"* the voice droned on, *"was strong and healthy, with remarkably robust constitution."*

There was a long pause. Dutton waited, pencil poised,

but Damien had fallen into silence. There was a choking sound. Dutton looked up in alarm, to see tears of anguish on the priest's face.

"Oh, Father," he exclaimed, "what is it, what can I do?"

By the light of the flickering lamp, Damien's face had the look of Christ in the Garden of Olives. Damien breathed heavily, then opened the floodgates of his tortured soul.

"Brother," he began, "how can I explain it to you when I can't understand it myself? I know that soon I will be home with my dear mother. Before you came I had no one to turn to. I have suffered much through the years, long before this cursed disease took over. Much of this suffering I have brought on myself, for I am an obstinate man, and cannot suffer weaklings or fools easily, and perhaps, it is true that I should have taken better care of myself. But if I had I would have been doing less for those who needed me. For this I have done penance, God knows, in many ways. It has been a rough and tumble battle at times, with the Government, with the Bishop, especially his assistants, and even with my Superiors in my own Congregation," he added, sadly. "But I was prepared to bear the consequences if I could obtain what was needed for my poor afflicted. But what I was not prepared for and which has now come to light is the slander being written and hinted at about me . . . "

Dutton listened in silence. This was no time to comment. It was better that this be out in the open, that Damien's mind and heart be rid of the festering poison of hurt.

"When I first came here, there were those who could not understand the vow of chastity nor believe that a man, freed from the restraint of society, could long lead a celibate life. They spread rumors that I was sleeping with women!" Outrage was in his voice now. "I ignored it. I knew, and my God knew, that there was no truth in this. It was bad enough that outsiders, people of rival religions or no religion at all were saying this. But now, since my disease, even my own Brothers in Christ, who should know better! It has seared my very soul!"

There was another long silence. Reflectively, he again took up the charge, reasoning it out, less for Dutton than for himself.

"They say I am making a hero of myself, that I am not a good priest! But I don't understand. Have I not ministered to my people, baptized them, shared with them the Holy Mass and the Sacraments, prepared them for death? If people would make me a hero, it is not of my doing. If they have used my condition to better raise funds, must I be blamed? Ah, money! Useful, yes, but the root of all evil. Envy, personal pride, pique, who is going to administer this, who will decide that, who will have the honor here! That is the crux of the matter. But lies! Lies! Who can explain why they must lie about me! Take this down, Brother, word for word."

His voice was calm now, very deliberate, almost solemn, like a deathbed statement.

"Write, Brother: *'I have never had any sexual intercourse whatever!'*"

There was more dictation, about the first signs of the disease, about the remedies that Damien had tried when he privately judged he may have contracted it, down to when it became public knowledge. At last the document was complete.

At the priest's request, Dutton read back the entire text, Damien nodding vigorously at the part about his fidelity to his vow of perpetual chastity, as if to once more underscore the truth. The document passed up to him for a final scrutiny, he painfully inscribed: *"Correct: dated, March 10, 1889,"* and signed, with a flourish, *"J. Damien*

DeVeuster, Catholic Priest."

In the silence they turned Daisy around and headed back to the house. The moon was high in the heavens now as Damien was helped down. He rubbed Daisy's head, long and affectionately, caressing her velvety, quivering nostrils.

"Goodbye, old girl," he whispered, "you have served us well. God be good to you when I am gone." Dutton, moved to his very depths, watched Damien enter the house, then unhitched the horse. He lingered a long time before starting back to his quarters, staring silently at the moon. The end was not far off, he knew.

XI

The end, when it came, came quickly. The day after dictating his statement, Damien asked Dutton to record likewise his Last Will and Testament. There would be no further recriminations about money or the use of it. As a loyal son of the Church and his Congregation, he consigned all to the Bishop and his religious family.

His wounds were closing, the sores drying up—a sure sign that dehydration had set in and that death could come at any time. Still he hung on, indomitable to the last.

It was Holy Week, and there was much preparation for Easter. Brother Dutton was in his garden when a rush of footsteps caused him to look up in alarm. Himano was standing before him, in tears, not knowing how to say it.

"Oh God," Dutton breathed, "help us."

He dropped his utensils, brushed off his knees and raced to the house. Damien's room was filled with silently weeping friends. Mother Marianne and her Sisters were saying the Rosary as Brother James, supporting the dying man's head, wiped the death sweat from the face which, no longer swollen or disfigured, was even youthful in appearance. Dutton suddenly realized that Damien was a comparatively young man, only 49 years old, just three years his senior.

Father Conrady kneeling at the foot of the bed, began the prayers for the dying. Damien, comatose, still clung tightly to his crucifix with both hands. Gasping for breath from his race to the house, Brother Dutton dropped to his knees at the bedside. A smile crossed Damien's features. One hand groped searchingly and Dutton clasped it reassuringly.

At that moment, Damien gave a soft, almost imperceptible sigh and slipped away.

He was gone. It was all over, all the years of struggle and work, all the years of prayer and suffering, all the waiting, planning, pleading, all the years of hurt and misunderstanding.

Damien was gone. The great oak had fallen.

Book Three

———••●••———

After Damien:
An Awakened World

I

"Peace," Dutton thought grimly, "seemingly peace was buried with Damien."

The news of Damien's death had flashed around the world, intensifying interest in the "Martyr of Molokai." Gone were the hitherto comparatively quiet, purposeful days of building and teaching. There was no end to the avalanche of letters pouring in, asking for information, begging for pictures. Articles abounded, theories propounded. Visitors, bolder than some, came to stare, many to go back to write their varying, often conflicting impressions.

His correspondence, already heavy, multiplied as he tried, patiently and methodically, to keep up with this awakened awareness of leprosy in the modern world. But what shook him were the speculations about the character of his dead friend. "Off I am," he could still hear Damien's characteristic notification that he was leaving for another project, leaving him to pick up the pieces and finish the job. And "off he was" now, to the peace he deserved, but once more it was he, Dutton, who had to deal with the complications left behind.

He missed him sorely. All the cleaning and scrubbing, putting the place into some semblance of order, could not offset the loneliness he now felt, especially in the evenings, which formerly they had spent in companionable silence or shared reminiscences.

The vultures Damien had referred to so darkly had swept in, for a fact. The shaky truce between the factions—political, sectarian, hierarchial, had dissolved on Damien's passing. New disputes were now fueled by the mounting interest and accolades for Damien, being interpreted by the various groups as personal affronts. As Damien's Congregation tried to secure its tenuous hold, the government, both from political and sectarian interests, sought greater control. In between, the uneasy Bishop tried to maintain the status quo, afraid that all the hard-earned gains of previous years would be lost with its consequent adverse impact on the general work of the Church and its acceptance throughout the Islands.

What distressed Dutton the most, however, were the speculations and snide remarks being circulated, finding their way into print. So it was with misgivings that he received notice of the arrival of a journalist, a certain R. L. Stevenson, with the announced wish of interviewing the man closest to Damien, which, of course, was himself.

The work had been going so well. The good Sisters had the girls well in hand over at Kalaupapa, and he had been given full charge of the boys here at Kalawao. All in all, counting the cottages for the able-bodied, the dispensaries and infirmaries for the very sick, the work houses, the special living quarters for the physicians and "clean" staff, priests, Brothers, Sisters, and layworkers, both at Kalaupapa and Kalawao, there were some 374 buildings. Quite impressive, he thought with some satisfaction, knowing how much he himself had put into restoration, in some cases, major repairs or even starting from scratch in others.

This is what the visitor would see. But could this man possibly visualize what had gone before, what had greeted Damien when he arrived! Was this journalist seeking corroboration of the gossip and the ugly hints being bandied around Honolulu? He thought uneasily of Damien's last testament, his impassioned denial of wrong doing. But if, through common decency, the subject was not brought up, how could he give lie to a question never asked? And, conversely, how could he explain away the crudeness and inadequacy that, despite heroic efforts, marked so much of what the priest had almost single-handedly accomplished!

"Well," he sighed aloud, "nothing is so harmful as a lie to cover the truth. I shall have to do my best, and let God manage the results."

Stevenson came and stayed a full week. Obviously a sick man, from the looks of him, perhaps tubercular. The face was sharp, the eyes bright and inquisitive. But there seemed no malice in the man, he decided, and relaxed, even allowing himself the luxury of humorous anecdotes of a harmless nature.

Stevenson had laughed heartily at the description of how Damien could make even mistakes turn out all right, at least so that the thing would work even if in a far different way from what he had first intended.

"Would you believe it," Dutton had confided, "when facing the end product he would grin a moment, regard it for a few more minutes, then rub his hands and say, 'Well, we can use it!'"

Stevenson had talked with many others, on both sides of the Island, occasionally coming back to Dutton. On the evening before the scheduled departure, Dutton tried to ascertain the general impression Stevenson was taking away with him. Dapper and fastidious, the man must have recoiled more than once. Did he attribute it as part of the permissiveness and carelessness of the priest, or did he charitably and more accurately see it as a natural way of life for the lackadaisical character of the Islanders, reinforced by their circumstances to live merely for the moment! Stevenson did not commit himself, but he did seem to appreciate Damien's good qualities, his generosity, his candor, and fundamental good humor. And with that, Dutton thought, he would have to be content.

When the moment came for farewell, however, Stevenson clapped him on the shoulder.

"Don't worry, Brother Dutton. Your friend Damien is a man with all the grime and paltriness of mankind, but a saint and hero all the more for that."

II

He plunged ever deeper into plans and work. He vowed he would make Damien's dreams come true. Construction was under way now for the new home for the orphan boys, a project that he and Damien had made part and parcel of those last months before Damien took to his bed. Henry P. Baldwin, a rich sugar planter in Honolulu, had visited Molokai on several occasions, once in company with William Smith, president of the Board of Health, and lastly with a Reverend Dr. Hyde, a Presbyterian Minister, also of Honolulu, the latter responsible for interesting many influential people to provide funds for one project or another at Molokai.

Baldwin, Hyde, Damien and Dutton had toured the "shantytown" of dilapidated and makeshift buildings at Kalawao. Recognizing the need for better quarters for the boys and older men, similar to the Bishop Home for girls which was nearing completion at Kalaupapa, Baldwin had offered to donate what was needed to construct such a home, provided, of course, he had added, that details can be worked out with the Board of Health. It was to be named the Baldwin Home, Dutton noted.

Many a happy hour had been spent working on the plans—he and Damien—waiting for the snags with the government to be ironed out. What a shame, he thought, that Damien had not lived to actually begin the project, but at least the Board of Health and Mr. Baldwin had left the building of the Home entirely in his, Dutton's hands. No suggestions, no stipulations, no questions. This was his challenge.

Thank God for the Sisters, he thought. I don't know how I could have managed if they had not offered to come over and help with my boys. Now I've got to figure out some way to move those bare, ugly rocks. I could use some of the ammunition I had at my command in Decatur, he thought, reliving the seldom thought of incidents of his Civil War days. He was so far away from all that now. He thought of all the brave men who had died, on both sides, and to what purpose! But the nation had survived. Who was it who had said, "Better one man die than the whole nation perish!"

It came to him later that evening. He had spent the time following supper, getting abreast of the accounts, determined to bring them up to date before allowing himself the luxury of delving into the batch of mail brought in by the latest steamer from Honolulu. Unbidden, the quotation flashed back into his mind: "Better that one man should die . . . " Of course, he now recalled, it was the argument of the Sanhedrin, justifying their case for turning Christ over to the hated Romans. He winced as he remembered how Damien had suffered, the scapegoat between the struggle for power and recognition of those vested interests involved with Molokai. He thought of the factions still circling uneasily around. There were the Fathers of Damien's Congregation, trying to oust Father Conrady who was not one of them; there was the new Bishop, setting up strictures to insure that the Sisters and their special Confessor not come under the control of the Fathers; there was the government, backed by the businessmen who had made their riches exploiting the resources of the Islands, more intent now on self-justification of their callous exiling of all afflicted to Molokai, regardless of their condition, their needs . . . better the innocent should suffer, than their vested interests. Damien's had been the voice in the wilderness, and he, too, could be sacrificed, in the name of a "greater good."

And here he was, reaping the fruit of Damien's sacrifice. He wondered, uneasily, if he wasn't already beginning to think of the Baldwin Home as "his" success, "his" project.

He methodically sorted through the mail—the newspapers here, the inquiries there, the parcels over to one side, the recognizable personal letters placed under his mother's picture to be read last—a little bit of self-discipline he still exacted of himself. He tackled the papers first, anxious to have any news of the progress towards annexation. Every morning, when he ran up Old Glory, he wondered how long it would be before his personal devotion would become the patrimony of all.

He opened the paper from Honolulu, the *Elele*. His eye was caught by the title over one, long article: *"An Open Letter to the Reverend Doctor Hyde."* What's going on here, he wondered. It was written from Sydney. He glanced down to the end, seeking the name of the author who, apparently, was quite upset. At the name "Robert

Louis Stevenson" he caught his breath. This was the journalist who had come to Molokai, shortly after Damien's death!

All else forgotten, he adjusted his spectacles, fearing the worst. Yes, it was about Damien. His eyes raced ahead, seeking some clue. He saw the words "dirty, headstrong, bigoted." My God, he murmured to himself, noting that there was a letter within the letter. Stevenson was publishing a letter written by Dr. Hyde! As he read the charges that had so infuriated Stevenson, his own blood boiled. He had thought Hyde was a benefactor of Molokai, even a friend of sorts of Damien.

Was Stevenson going to defend Damien against Hyde's slanderous description of a man who could no longer defend himself? Dutton mentally kicked himself for talking so freely with Stevenson. If only I had embellished a little to soften the picture, he thought, or taken the bull by the horns and brought up the subject of Damien's morals. It's too late now, he groaned, and read on.

"We are not all expected to be Damiens," Stevenson pointed out. *"A man may conceive his duty more narrowly, he may love his comforts better; and none will cast a stone at him . . . your church and Damien's were in Hawaii upon a rivalry to do well; to help, to edify, to set divine examples. You have (in one huge instance) failed, and Damien succeeded."*

Dutton nodded, approvingly.

"I marvel it should not have occurred to you that when you had been outstripped in that high rivalry, and sat inglorious in the midst of your well-being, in your pleasant room—and Damien, crowned with glories and horrors, toiled and rotted in that pig-sty of his under the cliffs of Kalawao—you the elect who would not, were the last man on earth to collect and propagate gossip on the volunteer who did."

"Damien has been too much depicted with a conventional halo . . . " Dutton smiled at this, knowing that Damien, if he had seen such a description, would have laughed uproariously.

"When I visited the lazaretto, Damien was already in his resting grave," Stevenson had continued. *"But such information as I have, I gathered on the spot in conversation with those who knew him well and long; some indeed who revered his memory; but others who had sparred and wrangled with him. . . . "*

Dutton paused and looked up, trying to remember if he had mentioned to Stevenson the one brief altercation he had had with Damien. He raced through Stevenson's description of Kalawao and its people, *"every fourth face a blot upon the landscape."* Exaggeration here, he thought, sheer journalistic license!

"I never recall the days and nights I spent upon that island promontory without heartfelt thankfulness that I am somewhere else, and observe: that which I saw and suffered from was a settlement purged, bettered, and beautified . . . it was a different place when Damien came there, and made his great renunciation, and slept that first night under a tree amidst his rotting brethren: alone with pestilence; and looking forward (with what courage, with what pitiful sinkings of dread, God only knows) to a lifetime of dressing sores and stumps."

Dutton put down the paper, his eyes smarting from reading the fine print, but moistened, too, by the rush of emotion that coursed through him. He took off his spectacles and polished them slowly. Who would have thought a defense of Damien would come from such a source! The man had a way with words. The letter fairly seethed with a fine indignation. But there was something more, he decided, a discernment and sensitivity which delved deeper than outward appearances. He adjusted his spectacles, picked up the paper, and ran his finger down the column to find his place.

"... *an open mind and capable of receiving and digesting a reproof if it were bluntly administered; superbly generous in the least thing as well as in the greatest, and as ready to give his last shirt (although not without human grumbling) as he had been to sacrifice his life ...*"

There followed a list of Damien's faults, as detailed by Dr. Hyde, and these Stevenson dealt with, one by one, with irony, sometimes direct counter-attack.

"*'Damien was coarse'... you make us sorry for the lepers who had only a coarse old peasant for their friend and father ... 'headstrong!' ... I thank God for his strong head and heart!*"

Dutton was thoroughly aroused now. He felt like cheering. He got up and paced the floor with excitement. He thought he had schooled himself to perfect self-control, even had congratulated himself that he was past being caught up in any overwhelming emotion. He found his fist clenched, and he pounded it against the palm of the other hand. He swallowed back a lump in his throat, polished his spectacles again, then sat back down at the flickering candle, leaning over to finish this remarkable letter.

"*'Damien was bigoted' ... in him, his bigotry, his intense and narrow faith, wrought potently for good, and strengthened him to be one of the world's heroes and exemplars.*"

Dutton could appreciate that as no one else could. Versed as he was in the example of his mother, his Anglican friends in New Orleans, his acute knowledge of the shortcomings of many who prided themselves on their "Catholicism," he had, more than once, seen bigotry. Damien's, he decided, was the more understandable. The next sentence caught his eye.

"'Damien was not sent to Molokai, but went there without orders'... do you really mean these words for blame?"

Dutton stopped, reflecting. He, too, had come "on his own"—no one had commissioned him. But what a difference between his case and Damien's. Damien, a vowed celibate, in the first flush of his manhood, with ten successful years of mission work behind him, voluntarily responding to the needs of those abandoned by everyone else—he, Dutton, a penitent, hoping to atone for wasted years. Damien had given up everything, to find toil, ingratitude, misunderstandings and even crucifixion of a sort; he, Dutton, giving up nothing, had found respect and personal peace.

"'Damien had no hand in the reforms'... I tell you that, to a mind not prejudiced by jealousy, all the reforms of the lazaretto, and even those which he most vigorously opposed, are properly the work of Damien... if ever any man brought reforms, and died to bring them, it was he."

Hear! hear! Dutton mentally cheered. How this man could find the vulnerable spot to dip his pen in it, unerringly.

"'Damien was not a pure man in his relations with women'... many have visited the station before me. They seem not to have heard the rumor. When I was there I heard many shocking tales, for my informants were men speaking with the plainness of the laity; and I heard plenty of complaints of Damien. Why was this never mentioned?"

Why indeed, thought Dutton. Not once had this ever been even hinted at to him, by Dr. Mouritz or any of the people. Only Damien, who had carried the innuendoes in silence until that night when he had dictated his reply. Of this Dutton was positive. Damien was making his last, definitive statement, on the very brink of death. It was in fact a death bed statement. Who could doubt the man's sincerity.

"I had heard it once before," Stevenson wrote. Dutton looked closer. *"There came to Samoa a man from Hono-lulu; he, in a public-house on the beach, volunteered the statement that Damien had 'contracted the disease from having connections with female lepers'; and I find a joy in telling you how the report was welcomed in a public-house. A man sprang to his feet . . . 'you miserable little ---' (here is a word I dare not print) if the story were a thousand times true, can't you see you are a million times a lower --- for daring to repeat it?"*

Dutton pushed back the chair violently. God in Heaven, was it going to come down to this! He knew the origin of the story well enough. There had been a priest, not on Molokai, but on the main Island, who had indeed forgot-ten his sacred vows, and took up a liaison with one of the Hawaiian women. His name was Fabien, which was something like Damien. He had been brought to court, but the case had been discreetly glossed over, and the man had dropped from sight. Not so the story.

Resignedly he read on.

"I will suppose—and God forgive me for supposing it— that Damien faltered and stumbled in his narrow path of duty . . . "

Dutton had to stop. No, whatever Damien's faults, women were not part of them. Perhaps he should pen a follow-up letter, bringing out firsthand testimony to the true facts. This was no defense. Stevenson was champion-ing Damien, but the lies were remaining unanswered, now being spread all over the world.

He rose slowly and walked over to the window. For a long time he stared out into the darkness. He, Dutton, who had played with wantonness, wallowed in indul-gence, now the object of respect; Damien, who had for-sworn all by vows came halfway around the world to help others find God, now, in death, the helpless butt of leering, scurrilous tales! Indignation suffused him. He swept the paper violently from the desk, glared at it with rage, then bent over and picked it up, to rip it to shreds.

He sank back into the chair, his head in his hands and cried—deep, tearless sobs which wracked him, body and soul—cried as he had not since, bottle in hand, he mourned the loss of Eloise—cried as he thought he could never cry again.

III

Something was radically wrong. Something had happened to Himano, changing this once gentle, shy lad. Dutton could not put his finger on it, nor the time and place when it had begun. There was a sense of furtiveness, almost a sullenness at times. The boys, too, were undoubtedly privy to something. He had noticed a snickering which always ceased abruptly on his appearance. Something was afoot and definitely he was going to have to get to the bottom of it, before whatever it was got out of hand.

He missed Damien who knew his people so well, who always had the answer to the "why" of things. There was so much under the surface which a newcomer would never fathom without a knowledge of these islands, of all that had gone before.

Some of it he had gleaned in his twilight conversations with Damien, who, though not interested in secular matters except insofar as it concerned his work for his afflicted, still had been able to fill him in on some of the conflicting forces which had so shaped Hawaii, its life and lifestyle, its politics, its religion with its consequent latent distrust of all outsiders, even those clearly intent on doing good.

In the brief span of seventy years since Captain Cook first set foot on the then unspoiled tropical paradise, Damien had told him, Hawaii had lost both its innocence and its autonomy. The white men, first acclaimed as gods, brought disease, guns, and factionalism. As more and more of their lands were alienated and its people debauched by alcohol, the Hawaiians' veneer of Christianity was often hard pressed to cope effectively with the solid core of ancient, trusted beliefs. Certainly in the few years he, Dutton, had been on Molokai, he had witnessed the uneasy play of sectionalism, the internecine, petty, struggles for power. One day, if he ever got abreast of all the things that had to be done daily, he would try to get to the truth of all these charges and counter-charges. He wondered if there were any books or articles available on the political history of Hawaii. Surely, with all the talk of annexation, he could come up with something.

But in the meanwhile there was the matter of Himano. Dutton, sitting alone on his tiny verandah before night set in, after a day of classes, dressing sores, and working on the roof of the church, flipped through the pages of some magazines that had come in last week. He couldn't be too careful these days. It would never do to give them over to the boys until he had censored each page. So many things were being printed which could be a source of sin for them. Of what value was it to build houses, bind sores and take care of bodies only to lose souls. And with that worrisome thought, he went inside to the open ledger, awaiting its daily entries.

Some hours later, the flickering candle burnt down to the holder, he was still at work. But his mind was on Himano.

IV

Moki was embarrassed. He quickly hid the magazine behind him as Dutton came up unexpectedly. He feigned a wide-open smile of innocence and helpfulness.

"What do you want me to do, Brother," he volunteered hurriedly. "A message over to the other side, maybe?"

Dutton was not fooled, but he decided against pressing the issue for the moment. Better to take these things slowly, he reasoned, or I could lose him altogether.

"Why, yes, Moki, that is exactly what I had in mind. I have been looking for Himano, but he has been strangely absent."

At the mention of Himano, Moki dropped his eyes, regarding his toes with undue interest. He twitched his shoulders uneasily, not daring to look up.

"What is it, Moki?" Dutton was puzzled at the boy's demeanor. "What's the matter, lad," he queried, reaching for him. But the boy backed away, his eyes now wide with dismay. In his panic he dropped the magazine. He stood, rooted to the spot, as Dutton leaned down, picked up the lurid piece of trash with its bold headings. "Where did you get this Moki," he demanded, as he noted the "naughty-naughty's" of that era: women in tights, cinched-in waists and overflowing bosoms! "Where did you get this miserable tripe?"

Moki stammered, then blurted out, "Himano, Father, Himano. He gave it to me. We're all taking turns," he hastily added, anxious not to be the only one in this predicament.

"How long has this been going on?" Dutton was stern

now, but not roaring in rage as Father Damien might have, Moki reasoned. Taking courage, he decided to make a clean breast of it.

"For many weeks now," he declared. "Himano says it is time we stand up to the white man who would decide what we can see and what we can't see. Himano says our customs, our ways of doing things were good enough for our ancestors, and good enough for us. He says our people were not ashamed of their bodies but took pride in them. He says the white man's religions are false. They fight among themselves and can't agree on anything. They cover up their women, then undress them with their eyes. They call themselves Christians, but in their hearts all is lies and lust." Moki was trembling now, more at his temerity than in fear of its consequences.

Dutton pulled the rigid figure to him, putting his arm around his shoulders, and looked Moki in the eyes. "Is this what you really believe, Moki?" At the boy's barely perceptible shake of his head, he probed, "And why does Himano say these things? Why is he so anxious to have you and the others take up the old ways?"

Moki was miserable now, but he could see no way out. "Himano says Father Damien was different. He was a white man, but he had made promises to God, and he kept them. But he understood our people and he did not lie. He says you are a good man, too, even if you are white, but that you are bloodless. You do not know what it is to be free, to do what you want, to love . . . " His voice trailed off at the sudden fire in Dutton's eyes. From the surge of red that flushed the face, Moki thought Dutton was going to hit him, then realized that it was the effort of self-mastery which had gripped this man he had thought to be so cold.

"And Himano," Dutton pushed on angrily, "What about Himano? Does he know what it is to love?" He gave the boy a little shake, then released him. "Moki," he said, pointing to the picture of the dance-hall figure in its gaudy, seductive trappings, "it is true that nature, innocent nature is beautiful. When a woman is simply, modestly clothed, she is reserving the beauty of her body so that the beauty of her soul may be glimpsed in the purity of her eyes. But a beautiful body, half-clothed, reveals the evil in the soul of all who would seek to unclothe her further. This is what I have been trying to save you boys from. Do you understand that?" The boy nodded, not yet comprehending, but aware that Dutton was more grieved now than angry.

"Now, about Himano! When you see him, you may tell him that I want the rest of this from his own lips. When he is ready to talk, he can come to me."

Moki stared after the retreating figure, the clandestine magazine clenched under the unrelenting arm. Shaken and relieved that the confrontation was over, but aware he now must face Himano, he turned and slowly started towards the Home.

He sensed rather than knew, that fires were smouldering, like the gods Himano said were awakening in the seemingly dead volcano above.

V

The work was going smoothly enough, despite the constant changes in personnel and authority. Doctor Mouritz had gone, as had "Brother" James Sinnott. The buildings were springing up like mushrooms and he had the promise of four Brothers from the Picpus Order which would enable the Sisters to return to their work with the girls at the Bishop Home in Kalaupapa, as well as relieve him of much of the heavy work now claiming most of his time. More and more of the able-bodied were moving over to Kalaupapa, and, he was told, Himano among them. The grapevine had it that he was constantly in the company of a girl named Akala. She was among the more recent arrivals from Honolulu, and not at all like the usual Hawaiian women—docile, yielding. Rather she was pert and sassy, all fire. And she was full of ideas about revolt, about driving the Englishmen, the Germans, the French, the Portuguese, and, most of all, the hated Americans out of the Islands, to cling to the old Rule, the old gods, and the old ways.

Dutton had vowed he would never leave Molokai. He didn't even like to leave Kalawao, which he had only done in company with Damien when there was repair work to be done at Kalaupapa. Now he had to face it. He did have business in Kalaupapa, for there was the matter of shipping out Damien's effects and meager possessions to Belgium. But most of all, there was the matter of Himano, who had yet to come to him. If the mountain would not go to Mohammed, then Mohammed would have to go to the mountain, he decided quietly. And while there, he promised himself, he was going to see what he could find on the early history of Hawaii. Some of the current history, too, he amended, if he could locate a reliable source.

VI

At Kalaupapa, all was in ferment. Seeking authorization for the shipment and hoping to contact William O. Smith, his friend, who had shown interest in the Baldwin Home, he was told that Smith was no longer president of the

Board of Health, and was now a practicing attorney in Honolulu. He learned also that affairs in Honolulu were at a critical stage. Queen Liliuokalani, the ruling monarch, was beset from all sides, her decades of devoted church work forgotten in the screams of the "Reformers" who, under the pretext of saving Hawaii from the excesses of sovereignty, actually were setting the stage for annexation and total white rule.

This was news to Dutton who had fondly imagined that the people themselves wanted the security of annexation with the United States.

"I don't understand," he protested to Dr. Black. "Long before I came to Hawaii, I had read of King Kalakaua's visit to the United States and of his desire for American protection. Even before that, before the Civil War, the previous king, Kamehameha III had been negotiating for annexation as the thirty-second state."

The doctor smiled. "While you were fighting your Civil War, there was a war of another kind going on here. But it's going to take a little while even to begin to tell you about it. Are you going to be in Kalaupapa long? Where are you staying?"

Dutton did not want to embarrass the man by saying that though he had to be in Kalaupapa the following day also, he had no place to stay. He knew the feeling about anyone living in the settlement, and even the respect he knew he enjoyed might be sorely taxed when it came to any hospitality he might need.

"I have to be back in Kalawao this evening," he said, "but I plan on being back early tomorrow. Perhaps we can get together at a public house for a couple of hours?"

"Capital! I will try to get together some books and articles, and I'll be ready for you. These are trying times and it might help you to know more of what's going on."

Himano was nowhere to be found, despite persistent

inquiries. And all that evening, Dutton pondered the problem. One thing he had already learned disturbed him greatly. Opium was being slipped into Kalaupapa by merchant seamen, along with obscene art and suggestive, inflammatory literature. The afflicted, usually tractable even when not converted from their lackadaisical and licentious ways, were beginning to cause trouble. What had the boy gotten into!

The next day, his business concluded with the Board of Health, Dutton joined the doctor who had chosen a secluded spot in the rear of the public house. He was gratified that the doctor had not forgotten the promised books. There was also a half-dozen magazines, assorted charts, excerpts from the Hawaiian Gazette and heavily underscored reports. The good doctor must have been up half the night getting the information together, Dutton thought, and he thanked the man earnestly.

"You mentioned yesterday, Brother, that you were amazed at the idea of resistance to the proposed annexation. You couldn't understand the hostility to things American." He paused, selecting his words carefully, for it would not do to be quoted in any way which might show where his own sympathies lay.

"Perhaps it might help if I began with this chart." He pulled out a paper with a long line of figures. "Did you know that when Captain Cook arrived in Hawaii (it was called the Sandwich Islands in those days) he estimated the Hawaiian population to be between 300,000 and 400,000?" He smiled grimly. "That was in 1778. Your country was just breaking away from the colonialization of England. But all around the world, colonialization was the order of the day, and naval ships as well as merchant adventurers were plying the oceans seeking new ports of trade, new colonies. With these strangers came disease and death. The Polynesians were creatures of the land,

—95—

the sun, the water. They lived for the moment, were ingenuous and generous to the extreme. They welcomed the strangers, gave them their women according to time-honored custom . . . " He paused as he saw Dutton flush. "No," he said, anticipating Dutton's judgment, "they were not immoral, but rather amoral. They did not start from principles that are given to you and to me in our mother's milk!" He took a sip of his gin and tonic, regarding the fine features of this extraordinary man. Disciplined, yes, almost too much so, he thought, but a good man, not a hypocrite as many so-called Christians he knew.

Dutton drank a little from the tall glass of papaya juice he had ordered. He, too, was estimating the man before him. Cool and detached. He wondered what he thought of religion, if he had any. But the man was kind, and that covers a lot of sins, he reminded himself.

"But to get back to this chart," the doctor resumed, "only 45 years after Captain Cook made his estimation, which was later verified by many responsible chroniclers of his time, the population had declined to 142,000! Think of it, my friend," and the doctor leaned forward, indignation in his eyes. "Can you believe it? The prim New England missionaries clothed 'the naked savage' and their perspiration, instead of evaporating in the sun, soaked the miserable rags they were induced to wear day and night. The sailors brought syphilis, the missionaries brought tuberculosis. The Chinese brought leprosy. Measles, when it was brought in, did the rest." The doctor was trembling now.

"And that's not the half of it. Disease was bad enough, but exploitation was worse. The New England missionaries were not bound by religious vows or even the need to assume the posture of poverty. They may not have absorbed the vices of the Polynesians but they sure as sin absorbed their lands! They established huge plantations, exporting pineapple. They stripped the forests of valuable sandalwood. They could not count on the happy-go-lucky Hawaiian for labor so they imported workers. These workers, Japanese, Chinese, and the mutinous sailors or wandering derelicts intermarried with the Hawaiians. Today, as we near the turn of the century, the population figures have increased, yes, but observe!" The doctor pointed to the chart and the column for 1893: "72,000 Japanese, 23,000 Chinese, 23,000 Portuguese, 13,000 Caucasians (American and English and some German), and 35,000 Hawaiians and *part-Hawaiians!* Part-Hawaiians, not even 35,000 Hawaiians! From 400,000 all Hawaiians to 35,000 Hawaiians and part-Hawaiians!" The doctor's face was suffused with outrage. "This is what a century of the white man has done to Hawaii!"

Dutton was shocked. The doctor drained his glass and sat silent, his fingers toying with the empty glass. Dutton was mute, his glass forgotten.

"There's more here," the doctor said, more calmly now, gathering the papers and books together. "But if you want to understand the political unrest, remember these figures, especially the 13,000 Caucasians. Half of these perhaps are Americans, but they practically own the islands. They also run them, in one way or another. And now they are trying to take them over completely. Aliens, yet they have succeeded in obtaining voting rights. Still citizens in one country, yet they can vote and determine the future of another! Have you ever heard of such a thing anywhere in the world?"

Dutton was embarrassed and unhappy. This was not his picture of his beloved country. But he was too polite to argue the point. Once again he thanked the man for all the trouble he had gone to, and thanked him, too, for the small library which was useless even to offer to return, once it had been in Kalawao. He made his way to the church and knelt there lost in thought. It wasn't that long since he had heard its bell ringing out over the waters as he waited to land! He had thought it was welcoming him to a land far removed from the follies and evils of man. He had been prepared for service to the unfortunate victims of a dread disease. He had not expected to find the world and its politics invading his very sanctuary. The Angelus began as he took the road back to Kalawao, this time in farewell. He hoped never again to set foot in Kalaupapa.

VII

"You wanted to see me?"

Himano was standing at the turn of the road. Surprised and elated, Dutton hastily jumped from the rig. Himano had not moved forward, just stood there, defiance in every line, a sleepy, indifferent sneer on his face. Dutton could hardly believe the transformation in what had been the open, trusting countenance that had so interested him on that first trip on this very road just a few short years ago.

This was a man now, of course, but that alone did not account for the slackness, the dissipation, the hostility mirrored in this face. The crippled, claw-like hands plucked carelessly at his ragged shirt. His eyes were pin-points, and a clammy sweat gave off a reeky, offensive smell—more of stale clothes than leprosy.

"Himano," Dutton began, "what has happened? Have you been sick? What can I do to help?"

Himano swayed, indolently, untouched by the concern in Dutton's voice. He gave a short, derisive laugh, regarding Dutton with something akin to contempt.

"You whites," he muttered. "You think we want your help! We can do without it. You're nothing but bad luck for us. Father Damien, we could trust. But he's gone. The rest of you"—he spit. "The rest of you are nothing but rules and more rules. Do this, don't do that. Everything that is good you consider bad. You whites have your public houses, but no, no, to alcohol for us. Love is sinful, drink is sinful, everything that helps us forget our misery is sinful. And why do we have this disease? There are some who think even that is a punishment for sin! Whose sin? The innocent babe at its mother's breast, the young girl whose love has been given to only one?"

Dutton was hearing it all over again. With the doctor, it had come out as outrage. From Himano it was anger, too, but tinged with hopelessness and despair.

"Himano, my friend," he pleaded. But Himano was having none of it. He turned and beckoned to a girl waiting in the bushes.

"Come, Akala," he called, "come meet the white man who would take Damien's place!" And, as the girl joined them, he pulled her close to him, his crippled hands stroking her hair. "Look, Brother, at my woman. Anything I want, she gives me. Do you not desire her? If I gave her to you she would give you anything you want because I have spoken."

Dutton backed away at the thought.

Mockingly now, Himano pulled the blouse from her shoulder. "Look at her loveliness, Brother. She is everything a real man could desire. We have no rules here, just time—time to laugh, to play, to love. And when we have done, she even has a potion to ease my pain." And he pulled from his dirty pocket a small paper packet. "After that," he smiled, sleepily, "after that, nothing matters." And he pulled the girl to him, running his hand up and down her back.

"Go back, Brother, to your monkish quarters. Run your bloody flag up the pole every morning. I spit on you and, if I could, I spit on your flag." And, with that, he turned with the girl and disappeared into the sheltering forest. There was a short laugh, a rustle in the shrubbery, a soft murmur, and Dutton fled.

His soul was in revulsion, as if, in a sunny garden he had lifted a rock to find a coiled snake. He didn't remember clambering back into the buggy. He didn't remember the landmarks he passed. He only knew he wanted to get back to the peace, the orderliness, the safety of Kalawao.

VIII

Rising early and running up the flag, Dutton stood respectfully at attention, his hand over his heart as he watched a stray zephyr pick up the folds to unfurl Old Glory against the sky. It was his morning ritual, his one concession to the world he had left behind. Some day, he was sure, it would be Hawaii's flag, too. But a sense of disillusionment had crept into his patriotism. It rankled there, taking the edge off every report filtering through, of the 'off-again, on-again, away-again' progress of those pushing for annexation.

His nights, since his return from Kalaupapa, were spent in reading. And as he read he began to think, not so much as an American, but as a bystander witnessing a tragedy he could not stop, a tragedy beginning in the Garden of Eden, a tragedy that could almost wipe out a paradise, given the serpent, greed.

He traced the progress of dissolution, as mentioned by the doctor. The coming of the missionaries, the advent of schools. That should have been a good thing, he thought. But it had robbed the Polynesians of their own culture, to provide only a thin coating of Christianity—a Christianity that embraced them, not as brothers and equals, but as inferiors, to be patronized and, eventually, in the name of "order," robbing them of their patrimony, even their own Rule.

There were rebellions against the royal family. There were disciplinary actions by outside instigators. Treaties were made and laws passed only to be voided. Catholic missionaries arrived and were greeted as opposition to the status quo. French battle ships arrived, to protect the Catholic missionaries who were, in effect, as much emissaries of their country as they were of God. Planters and developers arrived, securing large grants of land, eventually to take over from the entrenched New Englanders, economics usurping the power of the Bible.

Dutton was fascinated by the play of power politics. French sabers and British flags, and always, in the background the forces of American money pushing the Hawaiian monarchy closer and closer to the edge.

It was not a pretty story and Dutton squirmed as he recognized much of the same pattern and even the same forces, France, England and the States, in what transpired during the Civil War.

"Money, money! Or is it power?" he cried to himself. "Money," he decided, "and what money will buy." Even the California gold rush had its repercussions on Hawaii. With gold so close, would not the mountains of Hawaii be equally a source? There was renewed interest by the French, the Germans were not far away, in Samoa. The Japanese still eyed the Philippines, the British were in Hong Kong. Unhappy at the prospect, the monarchy

decided to place itself under the protection of the United States.

And there the matter had stood, more or less, as first one force and then another prevailed in the ever shifting politics within Hawaii itself. During all this, factionalism was the order of the day as far as the rival religions were concerned. As one king died and the new one ascended the throne, allegiance would shift from America to England, and, with it Anglicanism would supersede the Puritanical New England Protestantism. With the Civil War in the States cutting the North from Louisiana's sugar, Hawaii's sugar business boomed, and, once again, America was riding high, its merchants in Honolulu now with dominant influence, effecting favorable trade agreements for their private interests, while slowly, inevitably tightening their control of the government.

Dutton was sickened by the intrigue, fascinated by the erosion of the Monarchy. He could not but conclude that, considering its steady decline and the paucity of its options, annexation was by far the best choice for Hawaii.

IX

One day was much like the previous day, and this was entirely satisfactory to Dutton. There was always enough to keep him busy. The Brothers had come, constructions had multiplied. He was getting older now, his hair dusting with white, his beard, somewhat fuller, already white. He had his boys whom he guarded carefully, mindful of Himano. The place was running like clockwork, with time to beautify and improve, even replace what had first been a filling of minimum needs. Only yesterday a shipment of trees had come in from Samoa which would keep him happily at work for days to come.

And the correspondence! It was increasing with every load of mail arriving from the States. Inquiries about Damien had abated, being replaced, often as not, by people he had never heard of, asking about him, Dutton! And people he had long ago forgotten were writing, some even asking to join him.

Dreams, he would think. They want to come ten thousand miles away to turn their backs on their problems. What they don't realize that once here, they're not ten thousand miles away any more, they're here. And their problems still with them, he chuckled. But he was always tactful in reply, suggesting gently that "Molokai is wherever you are . . . serve the people near you!"

What time he could spare from his ledgers and correspondence, he would spend on books, always his first love. He had read and reread all that the doctor had given him, augmenting it with every item that came in with the monthly mail. He had a much deeper understanding of Hawaii's history now, and a keener insight into its people, giving him a better perspective for the stories he wove in with the boys' lessons. They would listen spellbound as he would recount his experiences in the Civil War. To his accounts of the War between the States, he drew comparisons with what had happened and was happening in Hawaii. The rallying cry for the War between the States was, "Abolish Slavery," he explained. But the actual struggle was for added power in Congress, with the railroad magnates seeking to insure the dominance of non-slavery States as a balance against the Southern bloc, to advance financial interest in the ever-expanding drive of the railroads to the West. In Hawaii, he pointed out, the cry against the excesses of the monarchy masked the real motives...that of dominance and increased riches for those feeding the revolt. In both situations, he noted, the ultimate decision was in the hands of foreign powers. For the Southerners in America, it had been the loss of an expected ally, England, which had decided to drop the South to favor instead the colonially produced linen in preference to cotton, the South's only crop. Now, in Hawaii, it was a matter of foreign interests and their dreams for greater riches.

He buffered these stories of greed and power with explanations that it was not whole nations that were greedy, but the frailties of individuals that were at fault. Nations are good, he declared thinking in his heart of the United States, but sometimes evil people get control of the government.

So, while deploring the American hand that maneuvered Hawaii's politics, he could yet stand tall and proud, his boys around him, when, in July, 1898, news came through that Hawaii was at last a part of the United States, and they saluted Dutton's flag, now Hawaii's flag.

X

"You will not believe my temerity," he wrote to a friend. "I, who am nothing, with only a 1st Lieutenant, regimental quartermaster, in the war rating, have suggested, in the name of generating patriotism here, that the United States Atlantic fleet now touring Hawaiian waters perhaps steer a little off course so that our young boys can see the might of America." God forgive me for my pride, he chided himself. "I am told," he continued, "that this will take place, but I can hardly believe it, now that I think of it." He wished he had not told the boys until he actually saw the smoke on the horizon. What a disappointment if it all fell through.

"Brother Joseph! Brother Joseph! Come quick and see, they're coming, they're coming! Oh so many ships. I can see them!"

Dutton dropped his pen, letter forgotten. The boys were dancing up and down outside his door, not daring to take their eyes off the sight, but screaming for him to hurry.

"Brother, there's a million of them!" Ever the exact schoolmaster, even in his own excitement, Dutton could not resist correcting the exaggeration.

"Not a million, Pita! Not even Uncle Sam has that many . . . " But his voice trailed off. His hands were trembling. Pulling a large, crumpled, polka dot handkerchief from the pocket of his faded blue denims, he mopped his streaming face. "Now get in formation, all you boys. We must return their salute!"

It was July, 1908. Far off on the horizon, breaking the azure blue and turquoise of the Pacific waters could be seen a long line of ships, in battle formation. Unknown to Dutton, but aboard the flagship of the fleet, the Admiral's voice rang out: "We are now approaching the tip of the Island of Molokai. Some of you, perhaps, are wondering why we changed our scheduled course. Two days ago I received a message from President Theodore Roosevelt, instructing me to alter our course so that we might sail by this island. We are passing in review to honor one of the great men of our country. His name is Joseph Dutton. He is a soldier and a patriot, but more than that, he has given his life to work among those poor people who have leprosy. We will show our naval power to Brother Dutton and our friends on Molokai. We will dip our colors, and then continue on to Japan. Now, let's look smart and give him a real hero's salute! That is all."

The message was relayed to the other ships, (all four divisions), one by one as they sailed slowly by. All were displaying their full complements of pennants and battle flags. Battleships, cruisers, destroyers, with long lines of men in white standing at attention, rendering their salute as they steamed past.

He adjusted his binoculars. He could see the names now: In the first division, there was the S.S. Vermont (the State of his birth!), the S.S. Kansas, the S.S. Connecticut, and the S.S. Tennessee (where he was received into the Church). Then came the second division: the S.S. Georgia (where he had helped to save the Union), the S.S. New Jersey, the S.S. Rhode Island, and the S.S. Virginia. Then came the third division: the S.S. Maine, the S.S. Minnesota, the S.S. Ohio, and the S.S. Mississippi, followed by the last division: the S.S. Alabama, the S.S. Kentucky (he remembered those years at Gethsemani), the S.S. Illinois, and, the last, the S.S. Kearsarge.

Dutton and his boys stood at attention, heedless of the time ticking by. They hoped the men on the ships could see them lined up on the tiny knoll, and, high above, the Stars and Stripes dipping in return salute. With the last ship lost to sight on the horizon, there was a collective sigh as they turned, stiff and tired, but filled with an excitement that would stay with them for many days to come.

Dutton, back at his desk, picked up his pen. "They have come, and they have gone. What can I say, I am thinking to myself 'Did ever one deserve so little and get so much?' "

After that momentous event, Dutton received many letters from the officers and crews of the battleships. They told him how proud they were to be Americans when they saw him dip his flag in salute. Even President Theodore Roosevelt wrote to tell him that he, Brother Dutton, had honored America! That was most pleasing to the old soldier. It was an honor he would cherish more than any other he would receive in the few short years he had left.

XI

One day out of every two weeks heralded the arrival of the steamer bringing mail, sometimes a wheelbarrow full at a time, for Dutton. His interests and his contacts were spreading as more and more heard of this unique man on Molokai. And with Hawaii now a full-fledged Territory of the United States, with its own Governor, the U.S. Public Health took over Molokai, bringing, for the first time, American friends for the lone patriot. Now he had someone to share his excitement over each new advance, each development affecting either the mainland or his own remote island.

The building of the ill-fated U.S. Marine Hospital for research in Kalawao was, in itself, a small miracle for Dutton, especially since everything had been developing always towards Kalaupapa. The fact that it was erected on the very spot that Damien and he had projected for the Goto bath house made it doubly meaningful, a tie with the past and, he had hoped, an omen for the future. But the idea never caught on with the patients and it was to be closed. Mr. and Mrs. Frank Gibson, newlyweds, accepting the isolation of Molokai, had arrived to arrange for the gradual dismantling of the establishment, even running a post office of sorts.

Very strict guidelines had been in force and it was many a moon before either the Gibsons or Brother Dutton relaxed the prohibitions against the commingling of the personnel in the leprosy settlement and those working within the U.S. installation. Dutton received his mail from there and had frequent contact in passing, so that a friendship quickly developed. It was not until November 24, 1909, that he consented to leave the grounds of the Baldwin Home, for a Thanksgiving dinner with the Gibsons, and he had taken great care to be in a complete change of clothing, freshly laundered.

It was a memorable experience for him. He had not been at a Thanksgiving table or a meal in a "clean" home, nor even spoken to a "clean" white woman for more than thirty years!

Back in his own quarters what he remembered most, he thought, was the "rustle" of Mrs. Gibson's dress as she busied herself around the dining room. With a wave of nostalgia he thought of his mother, as he remembered her from childhood. He could see her, he reminisced, her curls escaping from the bright cotton mop cap, her woolen skirt pinned back over her red flannel underskirt until it was time to leave the kitchen to sit at the table. How many, many years ago that was!

"Dear Next Door Neighbor" he began his note of thanks, that same night, before going to bed. And "dear next door neighbors" they always were after that, long after the U.S. Marine Hospital was abandoned and had fallen to dust, the patients having refused to stay in its hospital-like confines.

In the meanwhile Dutton continued to call for his mail. One day, to the surprise of all there was a huge box, damaged in process which, finally unpacked, revealed the remains of a floral bouquet, with a note from the White House. It was the Inaugural bouquet of Mrs. Wilson, wife of the new President of the United States!

XII

Money was pouring into Kalawao these days. It was pouring out, too. Dutton's boys, a whole new generation of them, were Americans now, proud of their country, and anxious to help others. With Dutton, they chipped in to help worthy causes around the world, particularly the Red Cross. They could not go to fight for their country, but they could and did help those who were in the trenches of France. He began by selling war bonds to the patients and staff. Improving conditions had brought opportunities for the more able-bodied to make a little money by fishing or farming, and others got small wages for helping with the grounds and buildings. The more educated worked as clerks and others as teachers. This money was usually spent on recreation, tobacco and candy. Out of Dutton's own pension, forced on him by the United States at the close of the Civil War days, only a thousand dollars remained. He would accept no salary or stipend for his work at Molokai. He took out all he had and invested it in his country's effort. His enthusiasm was caught up and between them all, Dutton, the patients and the staff pledged nearly $3,000 for war bonds and $6,000 for the Red Cross.

He cast about for some additional way to be of service, feeling he had not done enough. His possessions were so few. He eyed his binoculars. "Why not," he thought. "If the Government can't use an old dog, they might use his tricks. Surely the Service would be glad to get these." And off to the Washington War Department they went.

He was overjoyed, some months later, to receive acknowledgment from the Assistant Secretary of the Navy, a Franklin D. Roosevelt, assuring him that his binoculars were in use on a battleship. They were returned to him, together with a certificate, at the end of the war.

The fame of this generous, outgoing, intensely patriotic, God-fearing man was spreading far and wide. His heart was big enough to embrace the whole world. Senators, Governors, authors wrote to him. Presidents honored him with commendatory letters, first Warren G. Harding, then Calvin Coolidge. To those who would make him a hero, on a par with Damien, he scoffed. "The world is busy: it cannot bother with many heroes." He was forever playing down the idea of heroism in his choice of Molokai, claiming he had the best part, everything a man could desire, time to think, to pray, to help others, no worries for the future, no needs for the present, no need to dwell on the past. He was well content and thanked God daily for bringing him to Molokai.

Honors, when sought, flee the pursuer; but flee from the honors and they pursue. The world had caught up with the exile. President Harding wrote: "Only quite recently my attention was drawn to the fact that now, at the age of eighty, you are still carrying on such wonderful work and are still enjoying good health. It is difficult to realize that this is less than one of those miraculous compensations which come sometimes to men and women who make the supreme sacrifice . . . your work is not unknown, is not unappreciated; all over the world there are people who regard you and Father Damien as men whose lives have been well-nigh perfect examples of self-abnegation, sacrifice, and service."

A school, in Beloit, Wisconsin, was named for him, with the request that "you bequeath the past, present, and the future teachers and pupils of the Brother Dutton School, your spirit of self-sacrifice and zeal for the good of humanity." He was most struck by the fact that three veterans from his old regiment were present for the raising of the flag that he had sent.

He despaired of ever catching up with his correspondence, but when the suggestion was made that in view of his cataracts he should curtail answering all the letters flooding in, he laughed.

"Take time off?" He brushed the suggestion aside. "But time is all I have to give." Soon he gave up smoking his old pipe. "Takes too much time to fill it," he explained.

He was offered a typewriter, a fountain-pen, even electricity. All these he refused, saying what he had was good enough for him. But he did not turn his back on any new thing which would benefit his boys. Thomas Edison had sent him records and a phonograph, which he immediately put to use in the Baldwin Home. The telephone was already in use for inter-island communication or for contact with other stations on Molokai. He himself rarely used it, but he recognized and respected its usefulness.

One night he was awakened by a messenger telling him to come quickly to the Brother Superior's office, as someone was on the line at Kalaupapa and had to speak directly to him. He dressed hastily, all the while wondering what disaster this portended.

"Brother Joseph," the voice crackled over the receiver as he held it to his ear, "we have a message here from New York City. May I read it to you?" At his assent, the voice continued: "Just received a message from Pope Leo XIII to the Venerable Brother Dutton. The Holy Father confers most cordially a special Apostolic Benediction as a pledge of Divine Assistance. He has your radio portrait on his desk."

Dutton was so stunned, he could not respond.

"Are you there?" the voice queried. At his mumbled

assent, the voice concluded, "that is all. Good night, and congratulations, Brother."

"What does it mean?" Dutton asked as he hung up the receiver.

"It means, dear Brother, that the Holy Father has heard of you and has sent you a special blessing."

"But why me? The Holy Father honoring me? I'm not worthy!" And he meant it.

XIII

He squinted against the light bathing the church with its morning radiance. The air was sweet. A mynah bird, startled by approaching feet, protested noisily, to disappear with a fluttering of wings. The harmonium gave forth a tentative chord or two, then launched into a processional, and all eyes turned to the back of the church.

He was almost blind now, but he could see them. Moki, the boy, now a full-grown man, and, leaning on his arm and looking shyly up at him, the girl, Talitha, from the Sisters' school. Her eyes were moist with love and the knowledge that she was his beloved. She was dressed in a simple, pure white dress, softened by a touch of blue at the waist. He, Moki, was also in white, tall, proud, and obviously nervous.

Dutton smiled in recollection, recalling the confrontation, so many long years back, when the youth had to face up to his wrong-doing. Thank God, he thought, I did not lose him. The boy had turned out well after all, was a teacher himself now, and a good influence on the others.

Thinking about it now, he wondered if this wasn't the story of every life, in a way. A seed is planted, it takes root, it grows. It is buffeted by the winds, sometimes crushed to the ground, but there comes the crucial moment which determines all the rest of its future. Will it have the strength to rise, take on new life and eventually blossom in the sun, or will it remain supine, to be trampled and rot in the mud. Moki and Himano. This could have been the story of his own life, he mused. But for the grace of God.

The couple were at the altar now. The music had stopped, and Father was interrogating them. "Moki, do you take this woman, Talitha, to be your lawfully wedded wife?" God, he thought, for the first time in many years, "Ira, do you take this woman, Eloise, for your lawfully wedded wife?" That was legal, all right, he had seen to that, but was it a marriage?

"Talitha," the priest continued, "do you take Moki, for your lawfully wedded spouse? . . . to honor and obey, in sickness and in health, 'til death do you part?"

Dutton's attention was brought back to the present. What a special meaning these words had for this couple. Sickness was not some "over the hill, far away in the future prospect" but a reality at their door. It was a pledge to life against the background of death. But then, death is sometimes long coming, he thought. Who would have thought he would still be here, deaf and half-blind, well into his eighties. God has been very good to me, he marveled. He had seen many changes at Molokai in the past four decades, had a hand in a few, he acknowledged to himself. And here he was, almost at the end of the trail, and God was now granting him this consolation of seeing some fruit of all these years with his boys. How unfathomable are your ways, O Lord, he prayed.

There was movement now at the altar. The couple had turned and were coming towards him, beaming with happiness. Diseased they both were, he knew, but there was no imperfection in them in the overriding beauty and love enveloping them. He felt his old heart would burst. Moki had been saved from lust, now to enjoy the bliss of pure love. Soon there would be a little Joseph or Josefina running around. When I go, O Lord, he breathed, may there be sons of my soul to pray for me, your unworthy servant.

XIV

A storm was brewing, the air hot, sultry and menacingly quiet. Dutton, taking a catnap on his verandah awoke with a start. The wind was sweeping furiously around his house, and, deaf as he was, he could hear the howling as the gale went into full force.

"The flag," he cried, "the flag!" But there was no one in sight. With no thought but to save Old Glory, he pushed his way from the porch, falling heavily, but rising enough to crawl slowly, laboriously down the path, up the little knoll, to the foot of the flag pole, He could not see the cord, but he found it by clinging to the pole and groping around.

The flag was whipping furiously in the wind, the cord wet and almost unmanageable. But somehow he eased it down, and clutched it, a sodden, dripping mass, to his old chest before he slipped to his knees to collapse in sheer exhaustion. And there they found him, unconscious, the flag safe and unsoiled, in his arms. It was many a day before he could set foot on his verandah again. Pale and trembling, he was brought out at last, to enjoy the morning sun and to watch, from afar, the boys raising Old Glory again.

The long bout with pneumonia took its toll, however. And he had to acknowledge that his active days were about over. But why don't they leave an old man in peace, he fretted.

"But you should, Brother, you really should." The voice was cajoling him, urging him. They were talking about the wonders of a new operation for cataracts. He had no need to see now. Leave him in peace. There wasn't much worth hearing these days either. He liked being left in peace, to pray at times, to rest secure in the love of the good God.

Everywhere there was change. Aeroplanes were flying overhead. Automobiles were taking the place of the horse and buggy. The authorities were talking of desecrating Damien's grave, honoring him, they said, by transferring his remains to Belgium! Honoring him by ignoring his wishes! He knew Damien wanted to be where he had lived and worked, with his people. He fumed. He was going to make it quite plain he intended to remain on Molokai and be buried next to Damien where he had already laid out the plot, with Damien's consent.

"Really, Brother, let us take you to the hospital in Honolulu, if only for a few weeks. We'll see to it that you return, we promise you. It's not just your eyes, you know. The pneumonia nearly took you from us. You wouldn't want to collapse again and be bedridden for the rest of your life, now would you?"

That did it. He did not want to be a burden to anyone. But Honolulu? He did not like the idea of leaving Molokai for he had promised himself he would never step foot on other soil. But obedience was important, too, and example. He had always urged others to follow orders. Reluctantly, he gave in.

The rest was a blur, confusion, cacophony of voices, goodbyes, wailings, instructions, being lifted, beeps, bells, clanking chains, fog horns, the slap of waves he had long forgotten, more voices, more lifting, clanging, strange flashes of light, and finally, but finally, the reassuring pressure of the Sister's hand, the quiet peace of his hospital bed.

XV

Once again the ships were steaming towards Molokai. It was March, 1931. Once again ships were honoring the Yankee Dutton. But this time, he was aboard, in state, his coffin flag-draped, with an honor guard posted at head and foot.

The funeral had been a military one, a solemn requiem in the Cathedral, with the highest political and military officials joining with Church dignitaries to honor the layman Joseph. The Governor was aboard, the Navy officers, but no passengers.

Ashore, Old Glory dipped in salute, then settled to half-mast. Now he was returning to Molokai, as he had come so many years ago, to join Damien. He had been a lithe, still young man when he had first set foot on Molokai. That was almost half a century ago. The people waiting for him now on the shore were striking contrasts to the derelicts that had crowded around him, a stranger, that July morning in 1886. The scene had changed, too, from a creaking wharf, nondescript buildings and native shanties to imposing, well-kept government buildings, neat, painted bungalows. But the old pandanus tree was there, the tree under which Damien had spent his first nights, the tree which shadowed the grave Dutton had fashioned with his own hands for Damien, vowing to his fallen friend that he would remain to carry on his work. He had kept his vow. Now he was back to be buried in the same soil, to be one with his friend in their common sacrifice.

The end had come after weeks of debilitation, drifting in and out of reality at times. The cataract operation had been a success, and he could see after a fashion. But most of the time he spent praying, or, if approached, responding cheerfully, sometimes with anecdotes or shared remembrances. He was pleased whenever a card or message came in from friends, but his prayers, his rosary, his daily Communion was his life. He was, indeed, a man who walked with God, but a man who so valued others that he did not go to God alone—always he remembered others, to beg God's blessing on others. One of his last messages was "God bless them all, I pray for them all. I pray for the brotherhood of all men."

He liked very much Stevenson's poem, read to him one day:

"Home is the sailor,
Home from the sea.
And I lay me down with a will."

What was he doing here, in bed, when there was so much to be done and he sighed at the thought of the watery miles between him and Molokai. In his lucid moments he realized that death was not far away, but he was not afraid. "I lay me down with a will," he reflected. And he took comfort, too, when they told him his feet had not touched the ground since he left his little house at Kalawao. They had carried him to the ship and carried him off the ship. He smiled, gratefully, then drifted into a coma-like sleep. A few days later, after receiving the last sacraments, he lapsed into complete unconsciousness, from which he did not awake.

Now the old soldier was home, back on the soil of Molokai, back at his beloved Kalawao, back at the side of Damien. Everyone was there—old friends, co-workers, old boys and new boys. The priests were there, the Sisters, the Brothers. The doctors were all there, some who knew him, many who did not.

And Moki was there, holding the hand of little Joseph. And Talitha, big now with another child.

The prayers were over, the moment had come. The raised bugle glistened in the sun and the clear, sweet notes of "Taps" rose. Poignant, they hung on the air, sad, grave, bespeaking more the sorrow of the living than the glory of the dead. As the last note hovered with its long farewell, the silence that followed almost choked the throat with suppressed emotion. Slowly the multitude passed by the open grave, casting in a bit of soil, some adding a blossom as if to consign a bit of living beauty to accompany their friend into paradise. And then they were gone.

Over to one side, unnoticed, stood the wasted figure of a man with clawlike hands, hair wild and clothes unkempt, his gaunt face ravaged. For a long time he stared at the grave. Then, head bowed almost to his chest, Himano turned, his heart bursting with tears too deep to shed, and blindly retraced his faltering steps down the long, lonesome road from Kalawao.

Epilogue

Damien's body was indeed exhumed, to be transported to the land of his birth. His cause, too, was introduced, attesting to the extraordinary heroism and self-sacrifice based on his compelling vision of the Good.

Dutton, a man of altogether different vision, rests on at Molokai, no less a hero, no less a saint.

For sanctity is not pure, unadulterated worship of the Mighty, the Awesome, the Alpha and Omega of existence. It is the daily gift of self to all that God holds dear. It is a forgetting of self, really, to become totally absorbed in the Will of God, becoming an instrument of that Will, that all embracing Love.

Damien and Dutton, each in his own way, lived out their life for others. Theirs was the passion of people, that love of a motherhen for her chicks, that championing of the helpless, that empathy with the depths of true suffering without which all the so-called projects for charity are just passing pity, a pious preoccupation with "doing good."

Damien was accused of being a sinner, Dutton thought

of himself as being one. But if "sinners," the world has need of many more like them.

For their work remains. Leprosy is still the unconquered disease, affecting millions, misunderstood, its victims unduly ostracized, their future mainly without hope. Thanks to Damien and to Dutton, the world has been awakened to their plight.Laboratories have multiplied and research abounds as first one avenue, then another is explored for some possible solution to the enigma of leprosy. Treatments from the barbaric to the ridiculous have been discarded, replaced by oils, by baths, by potions and pills, by chemicals and their derivatives. The breakthrough is always just around the corner.

But in the meanwhile, the victim and his needs are with us. Advances have been made in rehabilitation and in opportunities. One by one, isolation—enforced settlements such as Molokai, are giving way to a more enlightened handling of those afflicted, and leprosaria, as institutions, are becoming things of the past.

Leprosy, however, is yet with us and the problems of its victims are acute. The closing of government-supported institutions means that funding must be found through private or sectarian efforts, if the work of research, rehabilitation and direct aid is to continue.

It is hoped this book, bringing to the fore the humanness of Damien, the "homeyness" of Dutton, the all-embracing charity of both, will focus the spotlight on opportunities for supporting the efforts of today's generous souls who walk in the footsteps of Damien and Dutton.

The steep black cliffs towered menacingly. This was the end of Dutton's long journey, and the end, too, of all that went before. This was his day of destiny.

The sound of a bell drifted across the misty waters, a mournful sort of welcome. Was that Damien's church? It was St. Francis of Kalaupapa. But it was St. Philomena at Kalawao, built by Damien, too, that he would come to love and spend his hours at prayer.

He had been told that Damien was a careless, slovenly man. Stepping into the church he had marveled at the exquisite cleanliness of the place. Everything bespoke the handiwork of a man who not only loved God but beauty as well. The interior of the Church of St. Philomena, Kalawao.

"This is called the Father Damien Road," Himano proclaimed loudly. "It was Father who built this so that we could travel between Kalawao and Kalaupapa and bring in the new patients."

"Is that Father Damien?" There could be no doubt. In the swollen features under the battered, broad-brimmed hat, was the man, barely recognizable, whose picture he had seen. This was the indomitable Damien.

Here he was, temporarily in Damien's spare room. The first thing he did was to take out the picture of his mother—and then the memories crowded in on him.

A scarlet bird, with shadings of blue and black outlined with yellow, pertly regarded him from the gently moving branch of a nearby tree. He must have looked like that the day he boarded the train to go off to camp. All brilliant plumage in the gaudy uniform of the Zouaves and full of confidence.

She had looked him up and down from the broad shoulders to his polished boots. He was clean shaven, and she was pleased by what she saw. Ira Dutton was a Lieutenant in the Northern Army during the Civil War.

He had thought that Gethsemani was the answer. He had tried for twenty months to succeed in doing penance for his past. Hours of prayer balanced with good hard work in the fields, and always the blessed silence. The altar of Our Lady of Gethsemani in Kentucky when Dutton was there, and (below) the Abbey as it looks today.

Damien was feeding his chickens. Dutton, watching from the verandah, could not take his eyes from the homey scene. The chickens were everywhere, running over his feet, one perched precariously on his shoulder. Was this the officious, overbearing, ruthless Damien he had been warned to expect?

"I was Joseph until I joined my brother, Pamphile at the seminary in Louvain. I took the name of Damien, the brave physician of Cilicia." Father Damien in the first days of his ministry, before he left for Hawaii.

"There's the question of a place for you," said Damien. "You should have your own quarters. A cottage with a combination bedroom and office and a flagpole in front."

"Makaio, my little one. Everything will be alright." He pressed the small, shivering figure to him.

Dutton seemed quite interested in the children, Damien thought. Perhaps this was the time to try to start a school.

St. Philomena
Church was origi-
nally built by
Damien. He wanted
to enlarge it and
make necessary
repairs and he turned
to Brother Dutton to
"complete the task."

"Hitch up Daisy, I
want to drive along
the shore." Dutton
took the reins and
gently walked the
faithful animal
down the rocky
road to the beach.

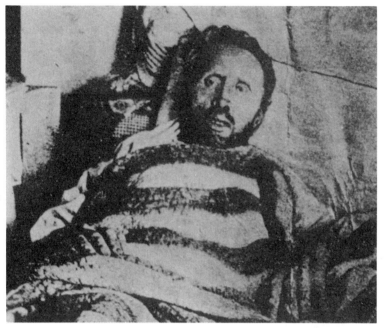

Dutton fell to his knees at the foot of the bed. A smile crossed Damien's features and then he was gone. The great oak had fallen.

"I am not an idle visionary, as some have undoubtedly judged. This is not a passing fervor which will vanish with the rising sun. I have sinned grievously against God, against others, and against myself. For this I am determined to do penance."

He was offered a typewriter, a fountain pen, even electricity. All these he refused, saying, "What I have is good enough for me."

The work had been going well. His days were filled with executing the plans for the new buildings to be known as the Baldwin Home. All in all, some 374 buildings were erected. Quite impressive, he thought with some satisfaction. If only Damien could be here to see this!

Robert Louis Stevenson watched him as he dressed the sores of the patients. He did not realize then that Stevenson's "Open Letter To Dr. Hyde," which would come later, would arouse such a storm.

The able-bodied had assembled for medicines for their assorted ailments. "There's more here than leprosy, they have their stomachaches like everyone else," Dr. Mouritz had said.

A long line of ships in battle formation was nearing Molokai to honor the Yankee soldier. Aboard the flagship of the fleet, the Admiral's voice rang out, "We are passing in review to honor a soldier and a patriot."

There was no end to the avalanche of letters pouring in, asking for information, begging for pictures. He worked at his desk by candlelight into the early morning hours trying to keep up with his correspondence.

The flag was whipping furiously in the wind, the cord wet, almost unmanageable, but somehow he eased it down, and clutched it to him.

"Really, Brother, let us take you to the hospital in Honolulu for a few weeks. It's not just your eyes, you know—the pneumonia nearly took you from us. You wouldn't want to be bedridden for the rest of your life." He agreed. He didn't want to be a burden to anyone.

Now the old soldier was home, back on the soil of Molokai, back at the side of Damien's grave. Damien, Belgian, priest, martyr of charity, and Dutton, Yankee, patriot, convert-penitent, now side by side, awaited eternity.

Questions
People Ask*

What is leprosy?

Man is the only natural host for the organism M. leprae which is the causative agent of leprosy. It is a chronic disease of nerves. It also attacks skin, and sometimes eyes and other organs. M. leprae is the only organism that is known to multiply within nerves. Nerves die and the areas served by them lose sensitivity. Thus leprosy is unique in that it can cause terrible pain, when nerves become inflamed, while at the same time it can cause skin to lose the sense of touch.

Why do people fear it?

In Old Testament times, many other skin ailments such as eczema, psoriasis, boils, scabies, and ringworm, among other things, were grouped together and called a common name translated "leprosy." Newer versions of the Bible refer more generally to a "dreaded skin disease."

How is leprosy contracted?

Scientists are still not sure. Perhaps since the bacilli are found in very large numbers in nasal passages they could be expelled and travel through the air. The unknown is one of the greatest barriers to the control of leprosy.

---

*Text and pictures with permission of Dr. W. Felton Ross, Medical Director of American Leprosy Missions, Bloomfield, New Jersey, and a recognized authority on leprosy. He took his medical and specialty degrees in England and served for nearly twenty years in Nigeria and Ethiopia.

Can leprosy be treated?

1. People rarely die of leprosy. But untreated, they slowly become more and more ugly and deformed.
2. People fear the unknown, and the cause of leprosy is known by only a few.
3. People commonly believe leprosy to be highly infectious. It is not. Most patients are not infectious. Infectious patients become noninfectious after a few months of treatment.

We do know that most people who associate with leprosy patients soon show evidence of resistance to the disease after a few months.

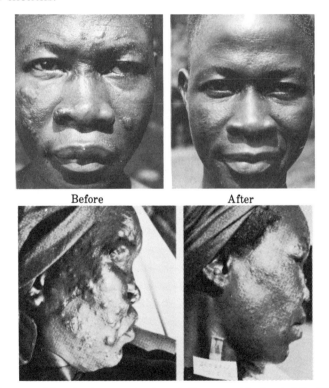

Before   After

Some need four to six years treatment. Some must be treated for life.

Leprosy can almost always be controlled and often cured, provided the patient is placed on treatment soon enough and his treatment continued long enough.

One of the sulfone drugs commonly used to combat leprosy is DDS. Not every case responds to DDS but it is still widely used as it is relatively inexpensive. Those patients who do not respond to DDS are given more expensive drugs, but many of these produce unpleasant side effects. None of the available drugs work quickly and treatment often takes years.

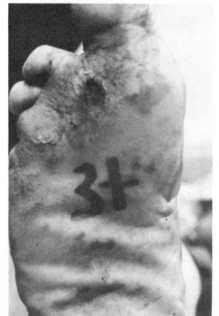

Leprosy damages motor nerves, thus causing paralysis.

Patients lose feeling in hands and feet, and as a result, injure themselves very easily. Injury and infection destroy hands and feet.

Good shoes can prevent and even cure some wounds.

Good leprosy programs, however, have often been the beginning of comprehensive medical care projects in which not only leprosy but many other diseases are treated.

Reconstructive surgery has been very helpful in those cases where deformities have occurred. However, those who have lost the sense of touch can never regain it. This makes the patient very vulnerable to injury especially when he feels no pain.

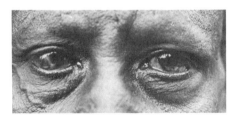
Some patients even become blind. But blindness is preventable.

One dramatic form of surgery is used to save the patient from going blind if he develops facial paralysis. Surgery may involve dividing the muscle to the jaw and running it under the skin to the upper and lower eyelids. The patient is then taught to blink by clenching his teeth.

How many have the disease?

About twelve to fifteen million.

Asia, India	6,475,000	Oceania	52,000
Africa	3,868,000	Europe	33,000
South America	358,000	United States	2,000

The World Health Organization estimates that only one quarter to one third of the world's patients are on regular treatment. The drug DDS is very slow and some patients need the much more expensive Lamprene.

What can I do to help?

Write to: The Damien-Dutton Society for Leprosy Aid, Inc., 616 Bedford Avenue, Bellmore, New York 11710.
Telephone: 516-221-5829.

The Damien-Dutton Society is a non-profit, tax exempt organization dedicated to providing funds for research, medical assistance, rehabilitation, education, and recreation for leprosy patients, regardless of race or creed.

About The Authors

THE SERGEANT, Howard E. Crouch, was born in New

Brunswick, New Jersey, but so long removed
as to be regarded a native to Long Island where
he has his home. He served in the United States
Medical Corps during World War II, three of
those years in Jamaica, West Indies, where he
became interested in the plight of the victims
of leprosy in the old "Lepers Home" on the
outskirts of Spanish Town. Among the staff of
ten Marist Missionary Sisters he met there,
caring for some 200 leprosy patients, men,
women and children of varying races and
creeds, was

THE NUN, Sister Mary Augustine, S.M.S.M., a former Wash-

ingtonian, who had relinquished a government
supervisory post to enter with the Marists in
the Boston area where she pronounced her
vows in 1939 in preparation for the missions of
the South Pacific. The attack on Pearl Harbor
cut off all contact with that area and she was
posted to the Caribbean for the duration.

The interest generated as the result of the Sergeant's personal concern for the patients led to his founding, in 1944, of an
organization to continue this work, which evolved into the
Damien-Dutton Society for Leprosy Aid, Inc., with headquar-
ters in Bellmore, Long Island, New York.

The war years over, he resumed his education at Columbia

University, earning two Masters degrees in Medical Administration, while devoting every spare moment to the development and growth of his leprosy aid group. Encouraged by a friend, he accepted a position in the Long Island school system teaching Advanced Placement Biology, which post he held for two decades, meanwhile serving as weekend administrator of Memorial-Sloan-Kettering Cancer Center in New York, from which he recently resigned after twenty years of unbroken service. Between teaching and commuting to New York, he continued promoting and developing the work for leprosy victims, his Society now aiding not just the patients left behind in Jamaica, but research, rehabilitation, educational and direct subsidy of leprosy projects around the world.

The Nun, likewise back in the States, for surgery, was assigned to promotional work for her community, finding time between editing and publishing, exhibits and speaking engagements, side courses in journalism at Marquette University, serving on committees and governing boards of national organizations, such as the Catholic Press, the Catholic Hospital Association, the President's Committee for the Physically Handicapped, and the Mission Secretariat, to assist actively in the development of the Damien-Dutton Leprosy Aid Society. Retired from her fund-raising efforts for the Marists, she has been allowed to devote as much time as needed to her first love, the leprosy apostolate, at present serving as editor of educational literature and director of the people-to-people correspondence program of the Damien-Dutton Society.

For more than thirty-eight years, the Sergeant and the Nun have worked in collaboration. Their first book, *Brother Dutton of Molokai*, published by Bruce Publishing Company, for the young reader, sold more than 20,000 copies before going out of print. With the fiftieth anniversary of Dutton's death now being observed, it is but fitting that a definitive story, in novel form, be made available as an invitation and a challenge to others to join in the conquest of man's oldest disease, leprosy.